Invasion of
the UFOs

Bethany House Books by

Bill Myers

Bloodhounds, Inc.
CHILDREN'S MYSTERY SERIES

The Ghost of KRZY
The Mystery of the Invisible Knight
Phantom of the Haunted Church
Invasion of the UFOs
Fangs for the Memories
The Case of the Missing Minds
The Secret of the Ghostly Hot Rod
I Want My Mummy
The Curse of the Horrible Hair Day
The Scam of the Screwball Wizards
Mystery of the Melodies From Mars
Room With a Boo

Nonfiction

The Dark Side of the Supernatural
Hot Topics, Tough Questions

Bill Myers' Web site: *www.BillMyers.com*

BloodHounds, INC.

4

Invasion of the UFOs

Bill Myers

BETHANY HOUSE PUBLISHERS
MINNEAPOLIS, MINNESOTA 55438

Invasion of the UFOs
Copyright © 1998
Bill Myers

Cover illustration by Joe Nordstrom
Cover design by Lookout Design Group, Inc.

Published by Bethany House Publishers
11400 Hampshire Avenue South
Bloomington, Minnesota 55438
www.bethanyhouse.com

Bethany House Publishers is a Division of
Baker Book House Company, Grand Rapids, Michigan.

Printed in the United States of America

Library of Congress Cataloging-in-Publication Data

Myers, Bill, 1953-
    Invasion of the UFOs / by Bill Myers.
        p. cm. — (Bloodhounds, Inc. ; 4)
    ISBN 1-55661-893-X
    [1. Brothers and sisters—Fiction. 2. Unidentified flying objects—Fiction.
3. Criminals—Fiction. 4. Christian life—Fiction. 5. Mystery and detective
stories.] I. Title. II. Series: Myers, Bill, 1953– Bloodhounds, Inc. ; 4.
    PZ7.M98234 Ip   1998
    [Fic]—dc21   00–504235
                                            CIP

For Danny Madrid.
A craftsman of skill and honor.

BILL MYERS is a youth worker and creative writer and film director who co-created the "McGee and Me!" book and video series and whose work has received over forty national and international awards. His many youth books include THE INCREDIBLE WORLDS OF WALLY MCDOOGLE, JOURNEYS TO FAYRAH, as well as his teen books, *Hot Topics, Tough Questions* and *Forbidden Doors*.

Contents

"I tell you the truth, whatever you did for one of the least of these brothers of mine, you did for me."

Matthew 25:40, NIV

1

The Case Begins

WEDNESDAY, 17:15 PDST

What was that?

Old Man Carlson jerked awake. The book he'd been reading clattered to the floor.

There it was again.

urmmm . . . urmmm . . . urmmm . . . urmmm

It was a low, rumbling sound coming from . . . coming from . . . where? He sat up and listened carefully. The noise was directly overhead. It was like nothing he had ever heard before.

urmmm . . . urmmm . . . urmmm . . . urmmm . . .

It wasn't an airplane. It definitely wasn't a helicopter. There was something very disturbing about it. Something

. . . *unearthly.* Mr. Carlson could feel the hair on his neck starting to stand up.

Across the room, he saw that his old tabby cat, Mrs. Tibbs, had also been awakened. She was backed into the corner, her tail twitching, her eyes wide with fear.

She let out a long, low growl. "Meowrrrrrr!"

As fast as he could, which wasn't all that fast, Mr. Carlson pushed himself out of the easy chair where he had dozed off and headed toward the kitchen window.

URMMM . . . URMMM . . . URMMM . . . URMMM . . .

The noise was louder now. So close it almost sounded like it was landing on the roof.

He pulled back the curtain. He peered through the window into the late afternoon darkness and let out an astonished cry:

"Eeeaghh!"

He wanted to turn away, to run for his life. But he couldn't take his eyes off the hideous creature that was staring back at him. It was awful. It had bugged-out eyes . . . crooked, yellow teeth . . . and wild hair that seemed to be growing in seventeen different directions at once.

Mr. Carlson moved closer to the window. As he did, the strange being on the other side of the glass also moved closer. He looked carefully at the thing. The thing

looked carefully at him. How weird. It seemed to be
wearing the same surprised expression on its face that
Mr. Carlson had on his.

Wait a minute. There was something else. Something
strangely familiar about this creature. . . .

Mr. Carlson reached up and smoothed his hair. The
creature did the same.

Next, he stuck out his tongue.

Repeat performance by the creature.

Mr. Carlson put his nose up next to the glass.

So did the creature. This was either the strangest case
of monkey-see, monkey-do or . . .

Suddenly he broke out laughing and shook his head
in embarrassment. "It's okay, Mrs. Tibbs," he called to
the cat. "It's just me." He chuckled softly. "I'm gettin'
scared by my own reflection."

But still, what about that noise?

urmmm . . . urmmm . . . urmmm . . . urmmm . . .

It seemed to be fading now. Moving north, toward
the hills at the edge of town.

He quickly yanked open the junk drawer and fumbled
for his binoculars. He found them and hobbled to the
dining room window, where he began scanning the
horizon for whatever it was that might be out there.

He was just about to give up when he saw them:
Three, no . . . four sets of lights moving silently across
the sky. They seemed to be attached to a round, metallic
disk. A disk that could almost pass for the flying saucer
he'd seen in last night's *Twilight Zone* rerun. And it
didn't look like it was just passing through. It looked like
it was actually getting closer to the ground . . . like it was
actually going to land in the nearby hills!

It was just as he had suspected.

The invasion had begun!

At that exact moment, just across town in Doc's
laboratory, Sean Hunter was doing what he did best . . .
complaining. "Nuffing hapng," he said as he tossed the
afternoon newspaper on the lab bench in disgust.
"Abfowutly nuffing!"

"What did you say?" his sister, Melissa, asked as she
turned toward him. "You sound like Elmer Fudd
speaking pig Latin!"

Sean swallowed his mouthful of chocolate chip
cookies and tried again.

"I said that there's nothing happening. Absolutely
nothing. Sometimes this town is so boring! And if we

don't find a case to solve pretty soon . . ."

"Yeah, I know. You won't be able to buy those new trucks for your skateboard." Melissa rolled her eyes and turned back to helping Doc with her latest experiment, a Holographic Video Display Camera.

Sean crammed another handful of cookies into his mouth and answered, "Muff moo mou mow mamout amyfing?"

Melissa turned back, waiting for a translation, but when she saw the chipmunk-full cheeks, the chocolate-smeared mouth, and the cookie crumbs covering Sean's shirt, she could only shake her head in wonder. "Do you always have to be such a slob?"

At the sound of that word, their one-hundred-two-pound bloodhound was up on her feet, trotting toward them.

"I'm sorry, girl," Melissa said as she bent down to pat her. "I said 'slob,' not 'Slobs.'"

But Slobs barely heard her. Now that she saw Sean, or more precisely what Sean was eating, she had only one thing on her mind. And if you couldn't tell by her constant whining and tail thumping, you could tell by her drool. Bloodhounds like to drool—a lot.

"Okay, okay," Sean said, trying to move out of her line of slobber. "I get the message."

The dog continued to thump her tail—and drool.

"Oh, all right," he sighed. "I guess one cookie won't hurt you."

He tossed the dog the last cookie, which she caught and swallowed in one gulp. When she was satisfied there was no more to be had, she turned and headed back to her favorite corner to resume her favorite pastime—sleep.

Melissa turned back to help Doc with a bunch of video thingamabobs, doohickeys, and whatchamacallits. (Melissa was never great at technical names.) "So," she called to her brother, "not much going on in town, huh?"

"Nah." Sean scowled at the paper. "Just some stolen cars and—oh, here are a bunch of kooks who claim they saw a flying saucer."

"A flying saucer?" Melissa exclaimed.

Sean shrugged. "Yeah, just some nuts. They probably saw that blimp that's been hanging around town the last couple days." He closed the paper and let out a sigh. "The point is, there's no work here for the Bloodhounds Detective Agency, and if you ask me—"

SNAP! CRACKLE! KAPOW!

Suddenly the room was filled with more smoke than the time Sean tried to barbecue. The reason was simple: Doc had just turned on the holographic camera.

Melissa turned to the woman. Since the scientist was deaf, Melissa quickly signed, "Is it supposed to do that?"

Before Doc could answer, the room filled with a swirling haze. First it was green. Then it was yellow. Then purple. Then all three colors at once. It began to take on a shape. And, even more frightening than that, it had a voice. . . .

"What . . . what's going off?" a scratchy, high-pitched voice demanded. A voice that Melissa immediately recognized—not only by the way it squeaked, but by the way it got its phrases mixed up.

"Jeremiah?" she called. "Jeremiah, is that you?"

"Misty?" he cried. "Misty, this is not my idea of a good dime!"

"You mean good *time*," she corrected.

"That either!"

Jeremiah was Doc's very first invention—a computer-generated character who could pop onto any computer screen, TV, or digital watch. Unfortunately, he was now popping into the room as a crackling, shorting-out, 3-D image that was at least nine feet tall.

He bumped his head on the ceiling. "Ow!" (Better make that ten feet tall.)

Slobs, who knew how Doc's experiments backfire, ran for cover, howling all the way.

Doc, on the other hand, did what any super-intelligent, super-trained scientist would do. She started hitting the back of the camera. But no amount of pounding worked. Jeremiah's image just kept towering above them, crackling and shorting out.

"What . . . what . . . what's happening?" the oversized electronic leprechaun cried.

"Jeremiah!" Sean shouted. "What did you do?"

"I was minding my . . . my . . . my . . . own business . . . and all of a sudden I'm . . . I'm . . . I'm . . . here, lifer than large!"

Sean and Melissa continued to stare as Slobs continued to howl and Doc continued banging on the video camera. Jeremiah took another step backward and hit his head on a chandelier, causing it to swing crazily.

"This is too weird," Melissa shouted. "A holographic image is just . . . an image."

Sean nodded. "But look what happened when he hit that chandelier. Images can't make things move! Somehow he's for real!"

"Of course I'm real," Jeremiah snapped. "I'm one hundred percent, solid state . . . state . . . state . . . circ-circ-circuitry." The poor fellow was popping and hiccuping like a . . . well, like a gigantic computer character that was popping and hiccuping.

Now he was holding a giant can of soda pop. And he was shaking it. "Hey there, boys and girls." Suddenly he sounded like a fast-talking TV announcer. "Have you tried the new and improved Cookoo Cola?"

"What's he doing?" Sean shouted.

"Sounds like a TV commercial!" Melissa called back. "Jeremiah? Jeremiah, can you hear me?"

But the giant image was too busy shaking the can and starting to open it.

"Look out!" Sean yelled.

Everyone ducked for cover, but they were too late. The cola gushed from the can like a giant geyser, spinning Jeremiah out of control and spraying cola all over the room.

"My hair!" Melissa shouted, trying to cover her head. "Look what you're doing to my hair!"

"If it doesn't g-get-get all over the place," Jeremiah sputtered, "then it doesn't belong-ong-ong in your face!"

"Jeremiah!" Sean yelled. "What's going on?"

"I du . . . du . . . don't know," Jeremiah cried, hiccuping and spinning crazily. "G-g-got milk?"

Now he held a giant milk carton and was spewing it everywhere.

Sean shouted, "He's stuck in some sort of TV broadcast space-time continuum!"

17

Jeremiah continued to spin faster and faster. Only now, instead of milk, the carton he held began spewing out . . . *basketball shoes!*

"Look out!" Sean shouted.

They dove behind the lab counter as shoes flew everywhere, pelting the counter, the walls . . . and exposed rear ends.

"Don't just stand there!" Jeremiah shouted. Now he sounded like a professional basketball player. "Beat the competition in Air Jeremiahs!"

Melissa stuck her head above the counter. "Jeremiah, you've got to stop this!"

"I can't!" the crackly voice shouted. He was picking up speed now—spinning even faster. "It just keeps on going." He panicked. "Going and going and . . ." The faster he spun, the higher his voice grew. ". . . going and going and . . ."

Until suddenly he was gone!

Just like that. No flash. No smoke. No nothing.

Melissa looked around and spotted Doc. The woman had managed to pull the power plug, and instantly the room was back to normal. There were no basketball shoes on the floor, no milk on the walls, and, most important, no Cookoo Cola in Melissa's hair. (She's a bit of a neat freak.)

Doc leaned against the counter, exhausted. Sean and Melissa rose to their feet and stared.

"I guess it must have been an illusion after all," Sean said.

"Yeah," Melissa agreed. "I hope the little guy is okay."

"No sweet," the familiar little voice chirped from a nearby computer.

All heads turned to see Jeremiah back in one of the monitors he called home. His clothes were smoking and his neon hair was still shorting, but for the most part he looked in good shape. "Actually," he continued, "I couldn't be bitter."

Melissa was sure he meant "no sweat" and that he couldn't be "better," but he looked so worn and frazzled she decided to let it go.

BRRRRP! BRRRRP!

Suddenly Sean's cellular phone began to ring.

He pulled it from his pocket and opened it. Then, trying to sound as grown-up as possible, he answered, "Bloodhounds, Inc. Private Detective Agency."

Melissa listened as he continued to speak.

"Uh-huh. Uh-huh."

"Who is it?" she whispered.

But Sean was too busy sounding important to answer her.

"I see," he said. "Flying saucers? How many? An invasion?!" His voice cracked, but he quickly brought it under control. "Yes, sir, of course we can handle that. Flying saucer invasions are one of our specialties. Yes, sir, you can count on us."

With that, he hit the power button, closed the phone, and looked over at his sister.

"Well?" she demanded.

"Well, what?"

"*Sean* . . ."

He broke into a grin. "It looks like we've got ourselves another job."

"What now?" she asked, already fearing the worst.

"Let's just say this one's really going to be out of this world."

2

Invaders From Where?

WEDNESDAY, 17:44 PDST

"Who was it? What did they say? Where are we going?" All of these questions and more tumbled out of Melissa's mouth as they raced down Doc's stairs and out the door.

"I'll tell you when we get there," Sean called over his shoulder. Without another word he hopped on his bike and took off.

"Will you wait up!" Melissa shouted.

But Sean wouldn't wait. He knew if he slowed down and stopped every time his little sister wanted him to, they'd never get anywhere. Girls—they could be such pains sometimes. He glanced down at Slobs running faithfully by his side. Why couldn't they be more like dogs? You know, always come when you snap your fingers, always obey when you give them orders, always chase after Mrs. Tubbs' cat when they see it. . . .

Always chase after Mrs. Tubbs' cat!

Oh no! But that's exactly what was happening. Mrs. Tubbs was out taking her giant, pampered cat, Precious, for an evening stroll. Of course, nobody walks a cat on a leash. Well, nobody except Mrs. Tubbs. And the sight of that fat, spoiled cat on her fancy little leash was more than poor ol' Slobs could take.

The dog went after her like a shot.

"Woof! Woof! Woof!"

Precious spun around and raced off . . . which would have been okay except for the part where Mrs. Tubbs had forgotten to let go of the leash . . . and the fact that the giant cat was a lot stronger than she was.

"Slobs!" Sean yelled. "Slobs, come back here!"

But Slobs had no intention of coming back. Precious was in the lead, with Mrs. Tubbs right behind, hanging on for dear life. And if that cat hadn't been dragging a frail little woman behind her, Precious would have set some sort of land speed record.

They dashed across the street, then around Mr.

Johnson's big elm tree a couple dozens times . . . as Mrs. Tubbs continued to scream.

"AUGHHH!"

Next, they headed for Mrs. Melman's prize petunias.

"AUGH! OUCH!"

Then into Mr. Ellison's cactus garden.

"AUGH! OUCH! AUGH! OUCH!"

And across the Corcorans' freshly fertilized lawn.

YUCK!

Actually, Mrs. Tubbs would have done just fine if it wasn't for the organic fertilizer, which was kind of smelly and . . .

KER-SPLAT!

. . . slick. The poor lady slipped and fell into the muck, face first.

DOUBLE YUCK!

"Mrs. Tubbs!" Sean yelled. "Mrs. Tubbs, close your mouth!"

Normally she would have taken his advice, but it's

hard to keep your mouth closed when you're screaming your lungs out.

And still Precious kept running.

And still she kept dragging Mrs. Tubbs.

"MOFFP!" the woman screamed. (It was supposed to be 'stop,' but as we've already said, her mouth was getting kinda full.) "MOFFP, PWOCIOUS! MOFFP!"

But of course, "Pwocious" would not stop. She had finally spotted a way of escape. Mr. Ellison's white picket fence was right in front of them. And, luckily for her, there was a board missing so she could just scoot through.

Well, lucky for Precious . . . not so lucky for Mrs. Tubbs.

"Not there!" she cried. "It's too small for me to—"

KER-WHAM!

Mrs. Tubbs hit the fence.

The good news was the leash finally slipped from her hands, and she came to a stop. The bad news was her wig didn't. It kept right on going, sailing through the opening in the fence and landing smack-dab in the neighbor's goldfish pond.

Sean and Melissa stared in amazement.

Not Mrs. Tubbs. "My wig!" she screamed, doing her

best to cover her nearly bald head. "My wig! My wig!"

Sean immediately moved to help. He leaped over the fence, dropped to his knees, and scooped her wig from the pond.

"Here it is, Mrs. Tubbs." He quickly brought it to her. "Good as new!" He hoped she wouldn't notice the dripping . . . or the slimy lily pad still stuck to it.

"Give me that!" She snatched it out of his hand and plopped it on her head.

But only for a moment. Because suddenly she went into another screaming fit and yanked it off. A shiny green toad sat atop her head.

It blinked once, croaked twice,

> "RIBET, RIBET,"

then hopped off.

Sean winced, waiting for Mrs. Tubbs to scream. But she didn't say a word. It's kinda hard to scream when you've passed out from shock.

When Sean and Melissa got to Mr. Carlson's house, he was out front, pacing back and forth.

"It's about time you got here," he said.

"Well, sir," Sean began, "we had a little bit of trouble with our dog, and—"

"Yes, yes! I see," the old man interrupted. "But we have to hurry. They've probably got their base half built by now."

"Their base?" Melissa asked.

"You know, to launch the invasion."

"Invasion?" Melissa was more than a little confused. It had been twenty minutes since the phone call at Doc's, and Sean still hadn't filled her in. "Will somebody please tell me what's going on?"

"Mr. Carlson saw an unidentified flying object," Sean explained.

"Unidentified, my foot!" Carlson practically shouted. "I saw a flying saucer. Flew right over my house and landed right over there." He jerked his thumb in the direction of the hills.

Melissa turned and looked. The hills were dark and silent against the night sky. Just for a moment, she felt a shiver run down her back. "UFOs? Here in Midvale?"

Sean nodded. "From what Mr. Carlson told me, I think the flying saucer he saw was the same one that was reported in the paper this morning. You know, the blimp."

"Blimp schlimp," the old man scorned. "This thing

came from Venus—I'm sure of it. That planet is really close to the earth this time of year. The saucer was big and silver and made this really weird sound. Scared Mrs. Tibbs half to death."

"Mrs. Tibbs?" Melissa asked.

"My cat."

"Ohh." Melissa immediately shot Slobs a look that said, *You'd better behave yourself . . . we've had enough trouble with cats for one day.*

Slobs wagged her tail and wrinkled her nose in an attempt to look cute and innocent, but Melissa wasn't about to fall for the act.

"Well, there's no use in us standing around outside," Mr. Carlson said. "You kids come on in the house. There's something I need to show you."

The front screen door creaked loudly as they entered. Slobs hesitated, but Mr. Carlson bent down and patted her on the head. "Come on, girl," he said. "We're going to need that nose of yours. I just hope you're good at tracking down space monsters."

"Mr. Carlson," Melissa began, "what exactly is it that you want Bloodhounds, Inc. to do?"

"What do I want you to do? Why, find out where that flying saucer has landed and do something to stop it!"

Sean and Melissa glanced at each other and

exchanged their world-famous *oh-brother* look.

The old man motioned for them to sit on the sofa as he hobbled over to his TV set. "I know what some people in this town think of me," he said. "They say I'm crazy . . . that I imagine things. And I guess I've given them some reasons to talk. But I didn't imagine that flying saucer. I was asleep in that chair . . . and it woke me up."

"Yes, sir." Sean nodded.

"But it doesn't matter if they won't believe me," Mr. Carlson said, " 'cause I know they'll believe you."

He turned to face them, then hesitated as if he had something else to say. Finally he spoke. "There's another reason I called you."

Melissa leaned forward to listen.

He cleared his throat and continued. "I knew your mother. Sometimes I'd see her in town, and she was always real nice to me. She never acted like I was crazy or anything like that. Your mother was a nice woman, and I was really sorry when I heard . . ."

His voice trailed off.

Melissa swallowed hard, trying to stop the tightness from swelling in her throat.

"Well, anyway . . . I figured I could do a lot worse than to ask her kids to help me."

It was touching to hear that Mr. Carlson had liked

their mother so much. But at the same time, it hurt to be reminded that she was gone. It had been only a few months since she'd died. Sometimes it seemed much longer, other times like it was just yesterday.

Melissa answered softly. "Thank you, Mr. Carlson." He nodded.

But Sean, never one to dwell on emotion, asked, "Now . . . what was it you wanted to show us?"

"This." Mr. Carlson turned back to the old TV and clicked it on. "Right after I saw that flying saucer, I turned on the TV to see if there was some news about the invasion. But there wasn't. Then something really strange happened."

"What's that?" Sean asked.

"The Martians started talking through my TV set."

"They did what?"

"They talked through my TV set. And I wouldn't be surprised if they're still doing it."

Once again Sean and Melissa exchanged looks.

But before they could say anything, the old TV set had warmed up, and they saw a very odd character with a high, nasally voice.

Suddenly Melissa burst out laughing.

"What?" Mr. Carlson asked. "What's the matter?"

"That's no alien," she giggled. "That's Steve Urkel.

He's supposed to be weird like that. You're watching a rerun of *Family Matters*."

"No . . . not him." Carlson shook his head. "Just keep watching."

A few more seconds passed before the picture and sound began to hiss and sputter as if something was causing interference.

"There!" Mr. Carlson pointed to the set. "Listen!"

Suddenly a strange and very mysterious voice began talking through the TV.

Melissa moved closer for a better listen. Was it English, or was it some weird space language? She couldn't tell.

"What are they saying?" she asked. "I can't under—"

"Shhh!" Sean motioned for her to be quiet. "Was that something about Saturn? Are they from Saturn?"

Then, just as quickly as it had appeared, it disappeared. *Family Matters* was back on the set and Steve Urkel was up to his usual antics.

But now there was a high whine coming from the opposite side of the room. Everyone spun around to see . . .

Slobs. The poor animal was whimpering as she stared out the screen door.

"What is it, girl?" Melissa asked, rising to investigate.

When she arrived she saw it. There, on the nearby hill, were a series of blue-and-white flashing lights. They were blinding . . . and like nothing she had ever seen before.

"What's wrong?" Sean asked.

But Melissa didn't answer. Oh, she opened her mouth all right, but no words were coming.

When Sean and Mr. Carlson rose and joined her side, they didn't do much better. In fact, Sean, who had a snappy comment for everything, only managed to squeeze out a faint, "Uh-oh . . ."

And Mr. Carlson could only get out two words. But they were enough to send another set of shivers down Melissa's spine.

"They're back. . . ." he whispered.

3

Dinner Anyone?

WEDNESDAY, 18:20 PDST

Sean and Melissa raced into their house and tore into the kitchen. The reason was simple: Now that Mom was gone, one of their chores was to fix dinner at night and have it ready when their father got home.

"Quick!" Sean shouted. "Turn on the radio and see if Dad's still at the station."

Melissa flipped on the radio just in time to hear their father's final words.

"And that's the latest news in Midvale. This is Robert Hunter at KRZY radio wishing you a pleasant evening. Good night."

"He'll be here in ten minutes!" Sean yelled. "We gotta move fast!"

"Gotcha!" Melissa yelled in agreement.

Now that Mom was no longer around, it seemed like Dad was having to do all of the extra work. That's why Sean and Melissa had agreed to help with the cooking. And that's why, at least for the time being, Mr. Carlson and the strange lights and voices would have to wait.

"What can we fix in ten minutes?" Sean asked.

"How about spaghetti?" she suggested.

"Good idea! That's fast . . . and easy. Get me a pot!"

"And how about some mashed potatoes?"

"Spaghetti and mashed potatoes! Sounds great!"

While Melissa looked for the pot, Sean also found a can of sweet potatoes in the pantry.

"What do you think about sweet potatoes, too?" he asked.

"I don't know. Sounds like a lot of potatoes."

"We'll put some marshmallows on top," he said, "like Mom used to do. We can tell him they're for dessert."

Melissa thought of arguing but knew it wouldn't do any good. Because once her big brother made up his mind, it never seemed to get unmade.

All in all it might have been a nice dinner. Well, except for three little details:

1. Sean didn't know how much spaghetti to use.

(He figured four bags ought to be enough.)
2. He didn't know how many marshmallows to put on the sweet potatoes. (But since four bags of spaghetti worked, he figured the same amount would do nicely for the marshmallows.)
3. He didn't know how high to set the oven. (But since there were so many marshmallows and since they were in such a hurry, he figured 500 degrees should do the trick.)

At first everything was under control. Spaghetti was in the pot. Sweet potatoes were in the oven. And Sean was standing proudly at the electric mixer making mashed potatoes.

"I don't know why you girls make such a big thing out of cooking," he shouted over the mixer. "This stuff's a snap!"

Melissa turned to him and was about to answer when suddenly she saw the stove. "Sean, the spaghetti!"

It was escaping—crawling down the sides of the pot and onto the stove.

He spun around and spotted it, too. "I must have used too much!" he shouted. "Put a lid on it!"

Before Melissa could obey, thick black smoke began pouring out of the oven. "The sweet potatoes!" she cried.

Sean looked worried now.

Melissa raced for the oven door and threw it open. Marshmallows were everywhere. Some were stuck to the sides of the oven. Others were on fire. But most were oozing and dripping out of the oven and onto the kitchen floor.

Meanwhile, the spaghetti continued to grow . . . covering the stove . . . wrapping around the radio . . . climbing into the crevice behind the refrigerator.

Sean moved to help but accidentally knocked the electric mixer he was using into *Ultra-High*. No problem . . . well, except for the mashed potatoes it began flinging around the room.

Splat splat splat splat splat.

The white goop flew everywhere—all over the walls, the counters, the windows. And of course . . . all over them.

Then there were the marshmallows . . .

And the burning sweet potatoes . . .

And the spaghetti . . .

"Don't just stand there!" Melissa cried. "Help!"

"I am!" Sean shouted as he desperately looked about the room. Decisions, decisions, decisions . . . With so many disasters it was hard to know which one to start with first. Unfortunately, Dad suddenly entered the room, saving him the effort.

K-THWACK!

That's the sound of an extra-big glob of mashed potatoes hitting the face of an extra-surprised father.

"What . . . what's going on?" he sputtered.

He was about to find out.

First, the spaghetti wrapped around his ankles, pulling his feet out from under him.

Wham!

He went down like a ton of bricks, flat on his back . . . right on top of the big, sticky pile of melted marshmallows. A pile so sticky that it would not let the dazed man get up. He tried once, twice, but was too stuck to move.

But he could still yell. "SEAN! MISTY!"

Sean was immediately at his side, dodging soft globs of flying potato. "Sorry!" he shouted. "We just wanted to surprise you."

Dad watched as the spaghetti continued wrapping around his legs, the oven continued smoking, and the globs of mashed potatoes

Splat splat splat splat splat

continued decorating the room.

"Well, son," he sighed loudly, "it looks like you've succeeded."

Less than an hour later, the family was sitting down to a scrumptious meal.

"I guess this turned out pretty well after all," Dad said as he handed out the cheeseburgers, shakes, and fries. "Sean, you want to say grace?"

Sean nodded and prayed. "Thank you, Lord, for Mickey D's . . . and that, uh . . ." He cleared his throat. "And that we didn't burn the house down."

"Amen!" Dad added with a little too much emotion.

Since the kitchen would still need a few more hours of cleaning, the three of them had decided to eat in the living room and watch a ball game on TV. But Melissa had only taken a bite or two of her burger before she asked, "Dad. . . ?"

"Yes, hon?"

"Do you believe in flying saucers?"

"Flying what?"

"You know, like UFOs and stuff."

Dad took another bite of his burger. He thought a

moment as he chewed. "Do you mean spacecrafts from other planets?"

Melissa and Sean both nodded.

"Well . . . no, I guess I don't. I mean, it's possible that God might have put life on other planets—the Bible doesn't tell us that He didn't. But if life does exist out there somewhere, I don't think they're visiting us."

Melissa felt the slightest trace of disappointment. "Why not?" she asked. "I mean, so many people say they've seen UFOs."

Dad nodded. "You're right. But did you know that about ninety-five percent of the time there's a logical explanation for what they see?"

"Really?" Melissa asked.

Dad nodded. "Weather balloons, meteors, satellites—they're usually things like that."

"But what about the other five percent?" Sean asked.

Dad shrugged. "Just because they haven't been explained doesn't mean there's something weird or mystical about them. It just means we haven't found the explanation yet."

Sean and Melissa traded looks.

Dad spotted them and asked, "Why are you two suddenly so interested in UFOs?"

Sean gave a loud slurp of his shake. "We got a call

from Old Man Carlson today and—"

"You mean Ben Carlson?" Dad asked.

"Yeah, and he—"

"I really wish you wouldn't refer to him as 'Old Man,'" Dad said.

"But everybody calls him that."

"Still, it's pretty disrespectful."

Sean nodded. "Anyway, he called us because he saw a flying saucer and—"

"Flying saucer?" Dad practically choked on a fry.

"Are you all right?" Melissa asked.

Dad nodded. "It's just that Ben Carlson calls the radio station at least twice a week with something crazy like that."

"He does?" Sean looked surprised.

Dad smiled. "Let's see. Last week he saw Elvis Presley down at Kmart. After that, he found some huge footprints in his backyard and was sure Bigfoot was in town."

Melissa and Sean exchanged another *oh-brother* look.

"Then there was the time he—"

"But, Dad," Melissa interrupted, "we heard the Martians talking on his TV."

"And saw flashing lights up in the hills," Sean added.

Dad hesitated a moment, then shook his head. "I'm

not sure what you two saw or heard . . . but whatever it was, I'm certain there's a natural explanation for it."

Sean let out a heavy sigh. "I figured as much. I guess we should never have taken on the case."

"Case?" Dad asked. "Mr. Carlson hired you to take a case?"

"He wants us to find the flying saucers," Melissa said. "Maybe we'll just tell him we're too busy."

Dad shook his head. "Oh no. If you agreed to take his case, I want you to stick with it."

"But, Dad—"

"Besides . . . Mr. Carlson is a very lonely old man. He doesn't have any family or friends."

"What's that got to do with anything?" Sean asked.

"Maybe if he had some friends to talk to, he would stop seeing Elvis and Bigfoot all the time. Or flying saucers."

"But we're detectives," Sean complained, "not baby-sitters . . . or old-folks sitters."

Dad reached over and put his hand on his son's shoulder. "I know you're detectives, but you're also Christians. And remember what Jesus said? 'Whatever you do for the least of these, you're doing for me.'"

BRRRRP! BRRRRP!

Sean's cellular phone began ringing. He grabbed it and answered, "Bloodhounds, Inc. Oh, hi, Mr. Carlson. Yeah . . . we were just talking about it. Oh really. More Martians up on the hill, huh?"

Sean couldn't help smirking.

"Uh-huh . . . they're making some kind of weapon. Right. . . . Yeah, well, Mr. Carlson, we're kind of busy right now, and—"

Melissa shot her brother a stern look. "Be nice!" she whispered. "*If* you know how. . . ."

Sean covered the receiver and was about to fire off a snappy comeback when, suddenly, a news bulletin came on their TV.

"WE INTERRUPT THIS PROGRAM TO BRING YOU A SPECIAL NEWS BULLETIN!"

All eyes shot to the TV. The ball game had been replaced by the local TV commentator.

"Good evening. Ron Dather with this live report from the hills just outside Midvale, where some people believe aliens from outer space have landed. Barbie Waters is out there now. Barbie, what's the current situation?"

"Well, Ron, I'm in the hills just north of Midvale, where . . ."

Sean, Melissa, and Dad sat stunned, watching the screen.

The local reporter stood in front of a small shack next to two strange-looking men who claimed to have seen the "invaders from space." One of the men was tall and skinny, with long hair and a scraggly beard. The other guy was short and fat. He wore bib overalls and a cap on his head that said *Joe's Worm Farm*.

"Yup . . . we seen 'em," the tall guy was saying. "They come right over our house there."

"'At's right." The short guy nodded.

Sean turned back to the phone still in his hand. "Er . . . Mr. Carlson? Something has come up here. Let me call you right back." He moved toward the TV for a closer look.

"We was just mindin' our own bidness," the tall guy continued, "when this big ol' saucer come whistlin' by. Scared us half to death."

"Shore 'nuff," his short buddy said. "Landed right over there. Then we seen this big ol' ugly-lookin' thing get out. About nine feet tall, I reckon. . . ."

"More like ten," the tall guy corrected.

"Yeah . . . ten. All green and scaly. Looked like a—"

"Frog."

"Yeah . . . like a frog. Or maybe a lizard. Anyway . . . tarnation if he didn't shoot at me with some kind a death ray." Short Guy pulled off his cap and stuck his finger

43

through a small hole that appeared to be burned into the bill. "I'd say we's lucky to be alive."

"You got that right," Tall Guy agreed. "I tell ya what. I wouldn't be comin' round these hills if'n I didn't have to. No way!"

The reporter spoke into the microphone. "And I understand that you actually got a photograph of this UFO?"

"Shore did." Tall Guy pulled a crumpled photo out of his hip pocket and handed it to the reporter. She took it and held it up in front of the camera.

"Can you get a tight shot of this?" she asked.

The camera moved in, shakily, for a better look. And there, on the ground, for all the world to see, was a small, circular . . . something. It was hard to tell exactly what it was, but it almost seemed to be glowing.

"That's it," Short Stuff said. "And that's me standin' right beside it. We only had a second—lucky the pitcher came out at all."

"Amazing," the reporter said. "What's this on the side—it almost looks like a rearview mirror—"

Tall Guy grabbed the photo out of the reporter's hands and crammed it back into his pocket. "Sorry 'bout that. But you wanna see it any more it's gonna cost ya. I mean, we might as well make a buck offa this. Right?"

The camera turned back to the reporter as she continued. "Earlier this evening, I had a chance to get some more reactions to this alleged invasion."

The picture cut to a father and his chunky kid, who was almost as round as he was tall.

"Hey!" Melissa cried. "That's Bear!"

"You're right," Sean agreed.

There on the TV was Bear and his father, Hank Thompson. They both wore hunting clothes and held deer rifles.

Bear's dad was the first to speak. "If these Martians think we're going to let them waltz right in here and take over this country, they've got another thing coming. Me and my friends are ready for 'em." He cocked his gun to show he meant business. "If they're looking for a fight, they're going to get it."

"And what about you, young man?" the reporter asked.

The camera tilted back down to Bear, who was busy cramming a handful of Chee-tos into his mouth. But that didn't stop him from trying to answer. "Mroff moph mufff mafferma . . ."

Yes, sir, there was no doubt about it—that was Bear all right!

Suddenly a pretty blond woman pushed her way into

the picture. She wore a long, flowery dress, and a huge crystal hung around her neck.

"We're so glad the enlightened ones have arrived." She almost seemd to bubble as she brushed the hair out of her eyes, and a hundred bracelets clattered on her wrists. "They've come to usher us into the new age of inner peace and tranquillity. And if they should be listening, I'd just like to say"—she grabbed the microphone from the reporter and waved her hand— "welcome, O cosmic ones! We greet you in the name of all humankind, and we await your intergalactic council!"

With more than a little effort, the reporter pulled the microphone back from the woman to continue the report. But it didn't matter. By now neither Sean nor Melissa was listening.

"Let's go!" Sean was already on his feet. "We've gotta check this out!"

It took more than the usual amount of pleadings and beggings with Dad . . . but at last they were able to wear him down. He agreed to let them go back out . . . as long as they cleaned up the kitchen first and promised to be home by 9:30.

That was the good news. But now as they stood all alone in the very same woods they'd seen on TV, there was a little bad. And it was tall, weird, and definitely unearthly . . .

"What is that?" Sean half whispered, half cried.

"Where?" Melissa asked.

"Over to the right. Shine your light to the right!"

Melissa spun her light around. It sliced through the darkness and came to rest on . . . not a creature from space, but an old rag caught in the branch of a tree.

"Whew!" Sean breathed a sigh of relief. He really wanted to meet up with aliens from outer space. But then again, he really didn't.

"Shhhh," Melissa whispered. "I think I hear something."

They froze a moment, but the only thing Sean could hear was the pounding of his own heart . . . and Slobs' nonstop panting. Until suddenly:

SCREEEEEEECH!

Melissa screamed. "What was that?" She spun her flashlight beam up into the trees.

"Only a screech owl," Sean answered. He did his best to sound bored, but he was grateful his voice wasn't as trembly as he felt on the inside. He continued up the

47

path, trying his best to keep up the cool, big-brother image. "We'll go only a little farther," he said. "If we don't find anything soon, we'll—"

"Look!"

Melissa grabbed his arm, and he let out a terrified scream.

"AUGH!"

(So much for keeping up the cool, big-brother image.)

"What is it!?" he cried.

She shone the light on the ground and kneeled down for a better look. "It looks like some kind of footprint or something."

Sean kneeled to join her. If it was a footprint, it was a big one. A *very* big one.

"Listen," she whispered.

"Now what?"

"It's too quiet."

Sean strained to listen. She was right. There was no sound. Nothing. Not even the sound of a dog panting . . . or drooling.

"Where's Slobs?" he asked.

"I don't know, I thought *you* were watching her."

"Me? Do I have to do *everything*?"

Even in the dark he could see her roll her eyes.

(Melissa was an Olympic eye-roller.)

"Slobs!" she called. "Here, girl!" She was half shouting and half whispering. "Come on, girl." She reached into her coat pocket and pulled out the crumbled remains of a cookie. "Want a cookie, girl?"

Usually the word *cookie* brought Slobs running. And with that nose of hers, she could smell a chocolate chip from half a mile away.

Suddenly there was a rustling in the bushes.

Sean and Melissa both whirled around. "Slobs? Slobs, is that you?"

But it wasn't Slobs. Instead, it was a couple of someones or somethings. Two very large someones or somethings that leaped out at them!

Sean tried to make a run for it, but he was too late. One of them grabbed him around the waist and held on tight. He struggled and fought but couldn't get away. "Run, Misty!" he shouted. "Run for your life!"

"I can't!" came her terrified reply. "They've got me, too!"

Almost Aliens

Several minutes earlier Slobs had stumbled upon a scent and was busy tracking it. She didn't mean to forget Sean and Melissa, but when bloodhounds track, that's all they think about.

The smell was everywhere around her—strange and yet familiar.

It was a people smell, except it was stronger than normal. And there was another smell mixed in with it. It was the greasy, pleasant odor that she often smelled on the kids' dad after he'd changed their car's oil. But it was odd for that kind of city smell to be out here in the woods . . . where you usually smelled grass, flowers, and the occasional bunny rabbit.

Still, it was on this bush here . . . that tree trunk there

51

. . . and these few blades of—wait a minute, where did it go? Oh yes . . . there it was, leading down the side of the hill.

Slobs started after it, then suddenly froze. Was that Sean's voice? Was he in some kind of trouble? She tilted her head to listen.

Nothing.

Figuring it must have been her imagination, Slobs turned her attention back to the scent and continued following its trail.

Meanwhile, with mouths covered, Sean and Melissa were being dragged through the night. It was too dark to see, but the opening and slamming of doors told them they were being taken inside some sort of building.

Of course Melissa was scared, but she was also angry. Whatever space creature it was that was dragging her away didn't even seem to care about her hair. Mr. Mutant from Mars was messing it up without so much as a second thought!

That's why, when the creature relaxed his grip, she let him have it . . . *POW* . . . right in the shin. (Or at least where a space creature's shin would be if space creatures had shins.) Anyway, the important thing was that her kick found its mark.

"Ow! Ow! Ow!"

The creature let her go and began doing a strange alien dance—hopping around on one foot in the dark and shouting, "Tarnation, Larry . . . she kicked me! The little brat kicked me!"

Tarnation? That didn't exactly sound like space-creature talk.

Somebody struck a match and swung it past Melissa's face, then Sean's.

"Why . . . it's only a couple a kids," another voice said.

The voice sounded familiar to Melissa, but from where?

"Kids? Are you sure?"

"They sure enough look like kids to me."

"Well, be careful, Roy," the other voice answered. "Space monsters can be pretty tricky."

"We *are* kids," Sean shouted from somewhere beside Melissa. "Honest! I'm a boy . . . and she's a girl. We're not monsters—we promise."

"That's right," Melissa agreed. "And if you don't let us go, you're gonna be in big trouble with our dad!"

The first voice chuckled. "Yup. They's kids all right. Now, just hold on fer a minute, you two, 'cause we was a-figurin' you to be Martians."

"That's right," the second voice explained. "They been givin' us enough trouble lately—buzzin' round here in their flyin' saucers, shootin' at us with their death rays. Shucks, we even been afraid to turn our lights on at night. But seein' as how you's just kids . . . I guess it's okay."

With the click of a switch, the room filled with light. Melissa found herself staring straight into the face of a short, fat guy wearing a hat that said *Joe's Worm Farm*.

"Hey!" she exclaimed. "I know you!"

"And I know you!" Sean said, pointing at the tall guy. "We saw you guys on TV."

"You did?" the short guy asked. "How'd I look?" He sucked in his stomach and put his hands on his hips. "You know, they say television makes you look at least ten pounds heavier than you really are."

"Now, Larry, it don't matter how you looked," the tall guy said. "The important thing is that we let people know about them flying saucers so folks won't come nosin' around these hills and gettin' theirselves into trouble . . . like these two almost done."

"You're right, Roy." Short Guy nodded and got a very

serious look on his face. "Listen, kids . . . I don't know what you're a-doin' up here in these hills, but it ain't safe. You better skeedaddle back on into town and don't ever come up here. You understand?"

"That's right," Roy agreed. "There's monsters lurkin' around in these hills. I mean, big ol' ugly things—look just like, like gorillas or somethin'." He put his hands high above his head and twisted his face into his best gorilla impression.

Melissa frowned. "But on TV you said they looked like frogs."

"Or lizards," Sean said.

"Uh-huh, uh-huh. Well . . . they kinda looked like lizards, and they kinda looked like gorillas. I guess I'd have to say they looked like *gorillazards*."

"That's right," Larry said. "And some of 'em is real small, too. We seen some strange things flying through the air about the size of a Ping-Pong ball. I guess you don't have to be real big to be a space monster."

Melissa glanced around the room. It was a hodgepodge of chairs and tables—none of them matched, and most seemed broken. In the far corner was a makeshift workbench, which was covered with oily pieces of machinery.

"What's all that over there?" she asked.

"That?" Larry asked. "Oh . . . well . . . that's . . . uh—"

"That's parts from a flying saucer," Roy answered.

"Oh yeah." Larry nodded. "You see, one of them kinda . . . uh . . . fell apart. I mean they was havin' some kind of engine trouble or something . . . and we was able to sneak up on it and get some of the parts."

"We got a pitcher of one. Wanna see it?" Roy asked. "Only cost ya a dollar!"

"We saw it on TV," Melissa said.

Roy was disappointed. "Well . . . that's okay," he said. "But let me tell you, we seen 'em swooping and buzzing through the sky like you wouldn't believe . . . and shootin' a death ray. Couldn't nothin' outrun 'em, neither. So what you want to do is go home and don't come back. And tell everybody you know to stay away from here. It just ain't safe!"

Sean nodded, but curiosity was definitely getting the better of him. He walked over to the workbench and pointed to one particularly oily piece of machinery. "What's this?" he asked.

"Go ahead, Larry," Roy said. "Tell him."

Larry cleared his throat. "Well, as near as we can figure it, that's a nuclear capacitor. From lookin' at that thing, we figure it helps 'em go about a zillion miles an hour. Prob'ly has somethin' to do with time travel, too."

"Really?" Sean took a closer look. "Looks like an old carburetor to me."

Roy laughed. "Oh no . . . that don't look like no carburetor, kid! You see—"

BRRRRP! BRRRRP!

Once again Sean's cellular phone began to ring.

Slobs stood on a small cliff, puzzled by the scene that lay before her. What were all those strange things below?

Some looked like cars. Then again, they didn't look like any type of cars she had ever seen. For one thing, there were no tires. And some of them looked like they had pieces missing. What in the world was going on here?

Brrrrp! Brrrrp.

Hold on! What was that noise? Slobs cocked her head and listened. Sean's telephone! For the first time since she'd picked up the scent, Slobs realized that the kids were nowhere around her.

She began to panic. What if her masters were in

trouble? With one swift move Slobs spun around and dashed off toward the noise as fast as her four giant paws would carry her.

Sean wasn't surprised to hear Mr. Carlson's voice on the other end of the line. The man had seen more strange lights in the sky and was hearing weird noises from the hills.

"Why don't you and your sister come over now so I can tell you about it? Maybe I could fix you some hot chocolate and—"

"Well, actually, Mr. Carslon, you see, um . . ."

As Sean tried to think up some excuse, Roy began showing Melissa more flying-saucer stuff. "Now, this may look like an ordinary exhaust pipe to you," he said, holding out a long piece of metal. "But we figure them Martians were a-usin' it to—"

Suddenly Slobs crashed through the door to save her masters. She saw Roy holding the pipe over Melissa's head and figured he was about to bonk her with it. So she immediately leaped through the air and hit Roy in the back, knocking him to the floor.

"Ooaf!"

Roy landed on his stomach, the wind knocked out of him. The blow knocked something else out of him, as well. . . .

His false teeth!

They went clattering across the floor, looking very much like a wind-up toy you might buy in any toy shop.

Slobs didn't know what they were, but she wasn't taking any chances as she followed them across the floor, barking and growling.

"My teef!" Roy cried as he scrambled after them. "Gib me my teef!"

Slobs swatted at the teeth with her paw and sent them flying across the room. They smacked Larry squarely in the behind . . . and stuck.

"Ow!" Larry shouted. "Who bit me?" He swacked and swatted at his bottom until the teeth were once again airborne.

"My teef!" Roy cried as he lunged to catch them. But they whizzed past and he missed. Once again he landed on his stomach, this time sliding across the floor. He banged into the wall, somehow managing to get his head stuck in a bucket.

Now dazed, he slowly rose to his feet (with the bucket still on his head) and staggered around the room. Red liquid dripped down the front of his shirt as he yanked and pulled at the container.

"He's hurt!" Melissa screamed. "Look at the blood! Look at the blood!"

"That ain't blood," Larry reassured her. "Them's tomatoes we just got from our garden. Roy, you silly fool! You're gonna ruin' 'em. Now, get that bucket offa yore head!"

"Mmfffmuffffflinhg," Roy cried. And then, unable to see where he was going, he walked right into the wall.

"Mowf!"

Luckily, he hit so hard that the bucket loosened, so he was able to pull it off. For a long moment he stood, covered in tomato paste, trying to regain his senses . . . until he saw his teeth sitting on the floor in the middle of the room.

Unfortunately, so did Slobs. She still hadn't figured out what they were, but they were definitely important to the big man. If she could just get them before he did, then maybe he'd start chasing her. And maybe this would give Sean and Melissa a chance to run away and escape.

Roy dove for his teeth.

So did Slobs.

But Slobs was just a little faster.

GLOMP!

She grabbed the teeth and shot out the door into the night. Holding them in her mouth, she looked a lot like the Cheshire Cat from *Alice in Wonderland*.

"Stob dat dog!" Roy yelled as he ran after her.

Sean, Melissa, and Larry were right behind. "Slobs, come back! Come on, girl! Come here!"

But Slobs was too busy saving their lives to listen. *"Slobs!"*

First she led them this way. Then that. Up this path. Down that one. Yes, sir, we're talking one very proud bloodhound. She ran just slowly enough that the bad guys would chase her, but just fast enough so they'd never catch her.

"My hair (*puff, puff*) will never (*puff, puff*) be the same," Melissa whined.

"Neifer (*puff, puff*) mill my teeef!" Roy groaned.

They took a sharp corner, then another, when they suddenly heard, "HALT! WHO GOES THERE?"

Everyone screeched to a stop. Suddenly they were in the center of a circle with a dozen rifles and flashlights aimed at them. The lights were so bright that it was hard to see faces, but Sean could tell they were men decked out in camouflage dress.

Slobs dropped the false teeth and began wagging her tail.

But one of the men aimed his gun directly at Roy's head. "Who are you people? What are you doing out here this time of night?"

Roy reached down, picked up his teeth, and wiped them off against his pants. "This here dog stole my teef," he said. "We wuz just trying to get 'em back."

"Um . . ." The leader didn't sound convinced. "What about this red goop all over your head?"

"Be careful, sir!" another man shouted. "It might be alien blood!"

Suddenly all of the rifles cocked as the men braced themselves.

"Hold it, hold it!" Larry cried. "It's jes' smashed tomatoes. Honest!"

"Smashed tomatoes?" the leader asked skeptically.

"Tha's right, jes' squished up and smashed tomatoes."

For a brief moment one of the flashlights caught the leader's face, and Sean recognized him. "Mr. Thompson!" The rest of the lights shot over to Sean. "Hi, remember us? I'm Sean Hunter, and this is my sister, Melissa. We know your son, Bear . . . er, I mean, Henry. We're good friends."

The man moved closer for a better look.

"Be careful, sir," someone warned.

"Oh yeah," Mr. Thompson began to nod, "I know you two. I think my son's been passing out some of your flyers." Everyone watched as he pulled a crumpled piece of paper from his pocket. "Bloodhounds, Inc. 555–2463. This you?"

"That's us!" Sean beamed with relief.

"Well . . . I'm sorry I didn't recognize you. But what are you doing out here? Shouldn't you be home at this hour?"

"Yes, sir," Sean agreed. "But we wanted to help find the Martians. That is . . . if there really are Martians."

"Keep up your guard, sir," the other man cautioned. "They still could be aliens, only disguised to look like the kids you know."

Bear's dad chuckled. "Oh, come on, Frank. Let's not get too—"

Suddenly another group of people came around the bend. There were about fifteen of them, weird-looking men and women, all carrying lanterns and singing songs. Some wore crystals around their necks. Others were dressed in flowing robes and had flowers in their hair. For the briefest moment, Sean wondered if these folks had been lost out here since the hippie days.

The leader of the group raised her hand. "Greetings! I

am Ramma Lamma. And these are my spiritual children." She swept her hand dramatically to indicate the crowd behind her. "Have you seen them? Have you seen the enlightened ones?"

Melissa tugged on her brother's elbow. "It's that lady we saw on TV."

Sean nodded. "And she sounds even weirder in person."

"Enlightened ones?" Bear's father asked. "I don't know who you're looking for, lady, but we're getting ready to blow a bunch of space monsters all the way to the next galaxy."

"Oh, you mustn't," she cried. "They have come to show us the way. They are not monsters. They are creatures of light!" She looked up at the sky with a worshipful expression on her face. "They have come to save the world."

Bear's dad shook his head. "They've come to make slaves out of us," he said. "And the first one I see, I'm gonna fill so full of lead that you'll be able to use him for a pencil."

Sean and Melissa continued to stare, unable to tell which group was the strangest. Unfortunately, it was at this exact moment that Jeremiah chose to make his appearance. Suddenly his little glowing body appeared on Sean's digital watch:

"Hey, guys, what's going off?"

Everyone in the group tensed.

"What . . . what was that?" Bear's dad demanded.

"That?" Sean asked, quickly shoving his hands into his pockets. "That was, uh, nothing . . . nothing at all."

"Hey . . ." Jeremiah's electronic voice squeaked from inside Sean's pants. "Who turned off the lights?"

"It's the Mothership!" Frank shouted. "It's calling them home!"

Once again Sean and Melissa found themselves surrounded by twelve angry men . . . who had twelve shaky rifles trained on them.

5

The Latest News
From Venus

WEDNESDAY, 20:08 PDST

Sean slowly pulled his hand out of his pocket. He wished with all his might that Jeremiah would just disappear. What would the little guy say in front of all these people? What could he do?

Fortunately, Melissa jumped in before he could do anything. "Looks like you forgot to turn it off," she said.

Sean looked at her, puzzled. "Turn it off?"

She gave him a forced smile.

Still not sure what she was saying, he decided to play along. "Oh yeah, turn it off. Right . . . sure . . ."

Melissa cranked up her smile even higher as she turned to the men and motioned for them to put away their guns. "It's only my brother's computer game." She laughed. "Pretty neat, isn't it?"

A wave of relief swept through the group, and several crowded in for a better look.

But as Jeremiah looked out and saw all the guns, he knew something was wrong. He didn't know what, but he didn't plan to stick around and find out. Instantly he disappeared from Sean's watch.

Everyone gasped.

Melissa shrugged. "It must have a short in it or something."

Sean nodded, doing his best to play along. "But I paid $59.95 for this thing!"

"If I were you, I'd get my money back."

"Good idea," Sean answered. "First thing in the morning."

That was all it took. Thanks to Melissa's quick thinking, the men with the guns had already lost interest in Jeremiah and the watch.

"Well . . ." Bear's father glanced at his own watch. "It's getting pretty late. And with them Martians or whatever they are out here, it ain't safe, so you kids best be running along home."

Sean and Melissa gave a grateful nod and quickly headed off.

As they entered their house that evening, Sean was still praising Melissa for her performance. "That was incredible," he said. "I've never seen you do such good acting!"

"Oh, it wasn't that great." She practically blushed.

"No, it's an amazing gift," he insisted. "The way you can suddenly look all innocent. I've seen you do that with Dad—turn on the tears and get your way with him. I mean, you've really got the knack for—"

Suddenly the living room was filled with light. "You two are a little late, aren't you?"

They spun around to see Dad standing in the hallway in his bathrobe.

Sean cleared his voice. "Yeah, I . . . uh, I guess we are."

Melissa, on the other hand, knew it was time to practice exactly what she and Sean had been discussing. Suddenly she turned on her most angelic look and answered, "We're sorry, Daddy. We didn't mean—"

"It's not going to work, Misty," he interrupted. "You're an hour late. You'd better have a good excuse."

Sean nodded. "Yeah, Dad, this time we've got a good one. Honest."

The three of them made their way into the kitchen and for the next twenty minutes, Sean and Melissa took turns telling about the night's events.

When they were finished, Dad sat in silence for a long moment. Finally he spoke. "You're right, something very strange is going on in this town. I mean, between these UFO sightings and the stolen cars—"

"Stolen cars?" Sean asked.

Dad shook his head sadly. "In the past two weeks, fifteen cars have been stolen in Midvale."

Melissa nodded. "Larry and Roy were talking about that on the way back. They think the aliens are stealing the cars. They think they're using auto parts to make repairs to their flying saucers . . . or to build some kind of death-ray weapon or something."

"That's crazy," Sean scoffed. "How could they build a death ray out of a bunch of old cars?"

Melissa shrugged.

Dad rose and pushed his chair back under the table. "When we talked about this before, I told you that I don't believe in flying saucers. I still don't. I'm sure that all of these lights and things people are seeing have a logical explanation. And as for those two guys you met up there in the hills . . . well, they've probably seen one too many Steven Spielberg movies."

He slowly crossed to the kitchen window. Sean and Melissa exchanged glances.

"Dad?" Melissa asked. "Are you all right?"

He nodded. "I'm not afraid of monsters from outer space. But I am afraid of nuts running around the woods with guns, ready to shoot at anything that moves." He turned to them and continued quietly. "I'm not going to forbid you to continue this case, but from now on you must be home on time—and you must be more careful."

"We will, Dad," they responded in unison.

"I mean *really* careful. Because if anything should happen to either one of you . . ." His voice trailed off, growing thick with emotion. It almost sounded like he was going to cry.

Melissa shifted. She didn't like this, not one bit. The only time she'd seen him cry was at their mother's funeral. She hated it. It made her feel so helpless. And it reminded her of how sad he really was.

He coughed slightly and, after a moment, changed the subject. "Oh, before I forget, Mr. Carlson called tonight."

"He did?" Sean asked.

Dad nodded. "Three times. Something about how you were going to come over but never showed up."

"We couldn't really help it, Dad," Melissa explained.

"I know. But don't forget about him, okay. Not just

because he hired you to solve this case . . . but because it will mean a lot to him to have company."

"Dad—" Sean started to protest, but Melissa cut him off.

"We know, Dad," she said. "Whatever we do for him . . . it's like we're doing it for Jesus."

Dad gave her a warm smile. "That's my girl."

"By the way, Dad . . ."

He turned back to her.

She swallowed and continued. "If you happened to have heard anything earlier about . . ."

"About you turning on the tears to get your way with me?" he asked.

Melissa lowered her eyes and nodded. Then she spoke. "I just want to say that—"

"Don't worry about it, hon." He yawned, stretched, and started for the stairs. "I didn't hear a thing . . . not a thing."

Melissa broke into a grin and raced up the steps. In a moment she was in his arms. As they stood on the stairs, holding each other, she could feel the moisture burning in her own eyes.

This time the tears were real.

THURSDAY, 10:00 PDST

BRRRRP! BRRRRP!

Sean sat up and looked around. For a moment he was still on board an alien spaceship. They had strapped him to an operating table and were tickling his feet with a feather duster as a part of their dastardly experiments.

BRRRP! BRRRP!

But if this were an alien spaceship, why did all the posters on the walls look exactly like the ones in his bedroom? Come to think of it, why did all the walls look like they were from his bedroom? And the ceiling . . . and the bed . . . and the—

BRRRP! BRRRP!

Wait a minute—this wasn't an alien spaceship! It was his bedroom. The alien scientists and feather dusters were just a bad dream.

BRRRP! BRRRP!

But what of that terrible noise? Was it a ray gun, a laser beam, a—

BRRRP! BRRRP!

At last Sean was awake enough to recognize the sound of his cell phone. He fumbled with it, got it up to his face, and spoke into the wrong end.

"Hello?"

No answer.

"Hello!?"

Still nothing. In a flash of genius, he flipped the phone around and heard perfectly. It was his old buddy.

"Oh hello, Mr. Carlson. Yes? What . . . of course . . . we'll be right over. . . ."

Two minutes later he was stumbling down the stairs, rubbing his eyes, and muttering about getting only eleven hours of sleep.

Dad had already left for work, but Melissa was in the kitchen, where she had been making an incredible breakfast of bacon and pancakes. As usual she was completely dressed, with every hair perfectly in place.

"Don't you ever get tired of being so neat?" he mumbled.

"Not as long as there are slobs like you to inspire me," she answered.

But Sean didn't argue. He knew that it was his morning to cook, and he was grateful that Melissa had decided to fill in for him.

She set a heaping plate in front of him, and he dug in.

It was pretty good. It was also pretty good not to see syrup all over the floor . . . or bacon grease splattered on the walls . . . or pancake batter on the ceiling. Yes, sir, as much as he hated to admit it, his little sister was definitely a better cook than he was. Not as exciting . . . but definitely a lot easier to clean up after.

Fourteen pancakes later (along with eight strips of bacon and three glasses of milk), he let out a loud belch. "That was great, Misty."

"Thank you . . . I think."

A minute later he was up and rummaging around in the pantry.

"What are you looking for now?" she asked.

"Oh, I just thought there might be some donuts—you know, for dessert."

"Dessert? With breakfast?" He could practically hear Melissa's eyes roll from across the room.

There were no donuts, but he had managed to track down a half-eaten package of Oreos.

"So . . . what's our plan?" Melissa asked.

"For starters, we've got to go by Old Man Carlson's house." Sean scarfed down another handful of cookies before continuing. "You know, he's really getting to be a pain. He called again this morning. Says the space people are talking on his TV again."

Melissa nodded. "I suppose we should go now and get it over with."

Sean sighed. "I just hope we're not wasting our time. Now that we know he's a nut, it might be better if we just went back to those hills."

Melissa shook her head. "We can't do that. Even if he is a nut, we have to be nice to him. You know what Dad says. . . ."

"I know, I know . . . 'whatever you do for the least of these.' " With a heavy sigh, Sean started for the stairs.

"Excuse me," Melissa asked, "where do you think you're going?"

"I'm going to get dressed. Why?"

"Aren't you forgetting something?"

Sean looked around the room. "I don't think so."

"Here. I'll give you a hint." She picked up the nearby apron and flung it across the room at him. "I cooked, you clean!"

"But I . . . I . . . I'm a guy."

"I know."

"But I . . . I . . . don't know how."

"I've visited your room. I know that, too."

"But I . . . I . . ." Sean was running out of excuses, and he knew it. "Misty . . ."

"Sorry, ol' buddy. Them's the rules." She gave a little

smile as she moved past him and headed up the stairs. "But don't worry, I think you look cute in an apron."

Mr. Carlson looked at his watch again. *Where could those kids be?* He thought about going to the phone and calling again, but he didn't want to be a nuisance.

The space people had been talking on his TV all morning, and the things they said were getting scarier by the second.

He hobbled into the bedroom and peeked under the bed to see if Mrs. Tibbs was still hiding there. She was. Poor cat. It used to be that she'd run and hide only when the alien voices interrupted the regular programming. But it had grown so bad that she didn't even want to be in the same room with the TV. All he had to do was turn it on and she'd hightail it out of there.

"It's all right, girl," he said soothingly. "Nobody's going to hurt you."

Mrs. Tibbs scooted farther under the bed.

Mr. Carlson sadly rose and headed back to his easy chair in the living room. He picked up the remote and hesitated. Should he or shouldn't he? But if the aliens were planning something, wasn't knowing better than not knowing?

He punched on the TV to see a rerun of *My Favorite Martian*. Perfect, just perfect. But the picture had barely come on before it grew fuzzy and the sound hissed and crackled.

Suddenly a strange voice spoke through the set. "It won't be long now," it said. "We're almost finished here."

"Yeah," another voice laughed. "Looks like this is one invasion that's going to go just the way we planned."

Meanwhile, Sean and Melissa pedaled their bikes toward Mr. Carlson's house . . . with Slobs running along beside. That's when Sean's phone rang again.

BRRRRP! BRRRRP!

For a moment he considered not answering it. It was probably just Mr. Carlson again. But remembering what Dad said about treating people with kindness, he figured he should at least be polite.

BRRRRP! BRRRRP!

He popped open the phone. Without even asking who

was on the other end, he answered, "We're on our way, Mr. Carlson, I promise."

But it wasn't Mr. Carlson. "Sean," the voice whispered. "Sean Hunter?"

"Yes . . . who's this?"

"Bear's father . . . Mr. Thompson. You've gotta help me," he whispered. "They've got me!"

Sean went cold. "Who . . . who's got you?"

"Please . . . you must come."

"Where . . . where are—"

And then suddenly—*CLICK*—just like that, the line went dead.

6

Galaxies of Fun!

THURSDAY, 10:42 PDST

Sean snapped the cell phone shut. He hesitated a second, then veered his bike hard to the left.

"What are you doing?" Melissa cried.

"Change of plans. Come on!"

"Sean!" She hit her brakes, skidded, and turned after him. "Sean, what's going on? Sean?"

"We gotta stop by Doc's house first," he explained.

"Doc's house?" she shouted.

"I'll explain when we get there. Come on!"

Once again Melissa was angry. Once again she felt left out in the dark. And once again she wondered why he was always so mysterious. Big brothers . . . go figure.

In a few minutes they had parked their bikes on Doc's

lawn and were racing up her front porch. But Sean hadn't even rung the doorbell before Jeremiah's high-pitched electronic voice barged in.

"Stop! Stop! It's too dangerous! It'll never work!"

Sean glanced at his watch and saw one very upset Jeremiah . . . which would explain why his little cartoon face kept changing from red to green to blue and back to red again.

"What's the problem?" Sean asked. "What's too dangerous? You don't even know why we're here."

"Oh yes, I do" came the nervous reply. "You're here for that 3-D TV camera, and I'm here to tell you it's too dangerous. And I should know. After all, once burned is worth two in the bush."

"That's once burned, twice shy," Melissa corrected.

"That's right!" Jeremiah bobbed his little head up and down. "And look before you lead a horse to water."

Again Melissa corrected him. "That's look before you—"

"Whatever," Jeremiah interrupted. "The point is you don't know what it was like to be stuck in that thing—to be blown up a hundred times your size, to be stuck doing bad TV commercials. . . ."

"Come on, Jeremiah," Sean tried to calm him. "You know how it is with Doc's inventions. They never work the first time. I'm sure she's got the wrinkles ironed out by now."

"Not this time." Jeremiah folded his arms across his chest in defiance.

"Jeremiah," Sean said solemnly, "I promise you that we'll be as careful as possible. But we have to use that camera so we can be in two places at once."

To further make his point, Jeremiah suddenly disappeared from the watch.

"Hey," Sean cried, "where'd he go?"

"He's probably off pouting somewhere," Melissa said. "He sounded pretty serious."

"Well, I'm pretty serious, too," Sean said as he reached out to ring the doorbell.

"I'm still not sure why we're here," Melissa said. "Will you tell me what's going on?"

"How many times has Mr. Carlson called us during the last two days?"

Before Melissa could respond, he answered, "Half a dozen."

She nodded.

"And how can we solve this case if we have to keep answering his calls and running back to his place?"

"But if Mr. Carlson finds some clues that are going to help us, shouldn't we—"

"We don't know if they're real clues or just in his head," Sean said. "But with the camera, we'll be able to find out."

He reached out and rang the bell again. "While he's recording whatever is going on at his house, we can go back to those hills and rescue Bear's father."

"*Rescue* Bear's father?" Melissa practically shouted.

"Oh yeah, I guess I forgot to mention that."

Melissa gave him a glare . . . which he did his best to ignore.

"You'll never get away with this!" Bear's dad shouted.

"Oh, Mr. Thompson, you sound like a very bad actor in a very bad movie. It's unfortunate you had to come snooping around here. You're almost as troublesome as those kids. But not to worry, I'll be dealing with them soon enough, too."

Bear's father sat in the corner, blindfolded, his arms and legs bound. They hadn't tied him up like this at first, but after they caught him on the phone . . . well, they weren't taking any chances. He didn't know where he was, and he didn't know who was holding him. The best he figured, it was the Martians, but for guys from outer space, they spoke pretty good English.

The voice continued. "We are making a few minor repairs to our flying saucer . . . including a fresh coat of paint. But tonight . . . tonight, we'll put on an aerial display the city of Midvale shall never forget."

Mr. Thompson couldn't help wondering about the word *paint*. Did they really paint flying saucers? And what was all that hammering and sawing in the background? It sure sounded like they were getting ready for something.

Suddenly his thoughts were interrupted by the crackling of a radio. Someone was reporting in.

"LITTLE GREEN MAN CALLING MOTHERSHIP. LITTLE GREEN MAN CALLING MOTHERSHIP. COME IN. . . ."

Once again Mr. Thompson fought against the ropes. He had to get away. He had to warn the others. . . .

It was past noon when Sean, Melissa, and Slobs finally reached Mr. Carlson's house. And as usual, he was waiting at his front door.

"I'm glad you finally made it!" he exclaimed. "They were talking earlier, then they stopped. Something about

little green men and motherships." He opened the door
for them to enter. "What's all that stuff you're carrying?"

"We hope it's going to help us catch those Martians
. . . or whoever they are," Sean answered. "I'll show you
how to hook it up."

Moments later he was attaching the video camera to
the TV set and explaining how it worked. "Keep the
camera attached just like this. And leave your TV on. If
the Martians should start talking, just press this button."

Mr. Carlson peered over Sean's shoulder and pointed.
"That button there?"

"No. Not that button. This button."

"That one?"

"No . . . no. . . . this one over here."

Carlson nodded. "Right. Got it."

"You sure you've got it?"

"Got it."

Sean had his doubts but continued. "This way we
won't miss anything. We'll go out and do our detective
work and then at the end of the day, we can come back
to check in and see what you've got on tape."

Mr. Carlson nodded. "Sounds good."

"Let's try it out to make sure it works," Sean said. He
flipped on the set and was greeted by the nine thousandth
showing of an *I Love Lucy* episode. The one where Lucy

and Ethel go to work in a candy factory.

But there were no Martians . . . at least for now.

Mr. Carlson practiced turning the camera off and on a few dozen times until it looked as though he was finally getting the hang of it.

"Nothing to it." The old man beamed. "But you two don't have to run off yet, do you? I'm sure the Martians will be back on the air soon. Can't you sit and talk for a spell?"

Sean looked at his watch, "We've really got a lot to do and—"

"Maybe you could have a donut with me."

"Donut?" Sean asked. (The man had obviously said the magic word.) "You, uh, you wouldn't happen to have any . . . Bavarian cream, would you?"

"Why, yes. Yes, I think I just might have one or two."

Suddenly it didn't seem nearly as urgent for Sean to leave.

But it was for Melissa. "I'm sorry, Mr. Carlson. Our friend's dad called this morning, and we think he might be in trouble."

Sean and Mr. Carlson sighed in perfect unison. Mr. Carslon because of loneliness, Sean because of the Bavarian creams.

"I'm really sorry," she repeated.

But of course she was right, and a moment later Sean, Melissa, and Slobs were heading for the door. In fact, Sean actually had his hand on the doorknob when Rosie O'Donnell suddenly began to go all squiggly.

"LITTLE GREEN MAN CALLING MOTHERSHIP. LITTLE GREEN MAN CALLING MOTHERSHIP. COME IN, MOTHERSHIP."

Melissa froze, then looked at her brother. "I know that voice."

Sean nodded. "Me too . . . but from where?"

They continued listening to the static-filled voices:

"MOTHERSHIP HERE. HAVE YOU. . . . zzzzt . . . buzzzzzz . . . MERCURY?"

"YES, SIR. IT'S ALL TAKEN CARE OF."

Mr. Carlson's eyes widened in surprise. "They must have conquered the planet Mercury!" he exclaimed.

"AND WHAT ABOUT . . . zzzzt buzzzzzzz. . . ?"

Sean crossed over to the TV and turned up the volume. "Man . . . I wish there wasn't so much static."

"Hssssss . . . zzzzzzzzzittttt . . . SATURN IS COMPLETELY DISMANTLED. NOT A PROBLEM AT ALL."

Mr. Carlson looked even more alarmed. "First they conquered Mercury—then they took Saturn! And now they've come here!"

"GOOD WORK, LITTLE GREEN MAN. AND HOW ABOUT THE GALAXY?"

"THE GALAXY WILL BE NEXT!"

Carlson slapped his forehead with his hand. "They're not going to stop until they've conquered the entire galaxy! We've got to do something!"

"WONDERFUL! OUR WORK HERE IS ALMOST DONE."

"BUT WHAT ABOUT ALL THOSE PEOPLE AND THOSE KIDS SNOOPING AROUND?"

An evil laugh sounded on the other end. And then came the ominous answer . . . "DON'T WORRY ABOUT A THING. AFTER TONIGHT . . . IT WILL ALL BE OVER!"

7

Please Don't Glow!

THURSDAY, 17:05 PDST

Several long and anxious hours had passed before Sean joined Melissa on the dirt road just below the hills. "Did you see anything?" he asked.

A tired and worn Melissa shook her head. "Not a thing. What about you?"

"Nothing," he sighed.

All afternoon they had been searching the woods, looking for any sign of Bear's dad. And all afternoon they'd come up empty-handed.

"I still think we should visit Larry and Roy," Melissa insisted. "You know, the guys from last night. Maybe they know something."

Sean shook his head. "If they'd seen anything, they'd have told folks by now."

"So where could he be?"

Sean looked back up into the hills. "I don't know, but it's getting late. And if those alien guys are planning something for tonight, I sure don't want to be out here when—" Suddenly he came to a stop.

"What is it?" Melissa asked.

Sean pointed down the road. There, coming up the hill, were Ramma Lamma and a couple dozen followers . . . complete with their crystals, rattling tambourines, and signs reading, *Please take me with you!*

Sean could only shake his head. "Will you look at that."

But Melissa had spotted something else. Coming up from the other side of the hill were another two dozen people—the wannabe soldiers from last night, complete with their camouflage clothing and rifles.

Sean whistled softly. "Looks like we're going to have a party."

Melissa nodded. "And someone invited *all* the weirdoes." She glanced around. "Sean? Sean, where's Slobs?"

Sean looked about and scowled. "I don't know. I thought she was with you."

Melissa shook her head. "I thought she was with you."

Sean raised his voice and shouted, "Slobs! Here, girl! Come on, Slobs! Where are you, girl?"

Halfway up the hill, Slobs stopped and listened. Sean was calling her. She turned her head toward his voice. She should go running to him—see if he was in trouble.

"Here, girl!"

He didn't *sound* in trouble.

She lifted her nose and sniffed. She didn't smell anything like trouble. And it was nothing like the strange scent she'd just picked up and had been following. The same scent she'd been tracking the night before. It was strong and fresh, and she really didn't want to leave it if she didn't have to.

"Here, Slobs!" Now it was Melissa's voice.

The big dog began to whine. She was torn between returning to her kids or following the scent. But in the end, it really wasn't much of a choice. After all, she was a bloodhound.

Slobs put her head back and let out a long, loud wail. There, if they were worried, that ought to let them know she was all right. She put her nose back to the ground, took another deep whiff, and continued running up the hill in the direction of . . . of . . . well, of something that smelled very, very strange. . . .

"Did you hear that?" Melissa asked. "It was Slobs. She was howling."

Sean nodded. "Maybe she's off chasing a rabbit."

Melissa fidgeted. "I don't know. . . ."

Soldiers and Ramma Lamma's group had met. Suddenly someone cried, "THEY'RE HERE! THEY'RE HERE! THE MARTIANS ARE COMING!"

Everyone turned to look as the person pointed up the hill to the left.

Sure enough, something was moving—way up high on the hill. You could see the flickering of lights . . . and you could hear the hum of strange electronic equipment.

"They've come to save us!" Ramma Lamma cried.

"They've come to enslave us!" Frank, the leader of the wannabes, shouted.

"Let me out of here!" another soldier cried as he dropped his gun and ran for his life.

Meanwhile, the sound grew louder and the lights grew brighter.

"Let's go show these outer-space creeps who's really the boss!" Frank shouted.

But Ramma Lamma was immediately in his face. "If you so much as touch one of them, I'll brain you!" she screamed.

"Brain me! You and what army?" he sneered.

"Me and this tambourine!" With that, she popped him a good one, right across the forehead. He teetered left, then right, then dropped to the ground.

Another soldier moved in, but she was ready for him, too. "I told you! They've come to usher in an age of lasting peace!"

BAM!

She got him right in the kisser, and he dropped on top of Frank.

Then before you knew it, a nasty fight had broken out. (And the guys with the camouflage and guns were definitely not winning.)

Sean and Melissa watched, amazed, as the New Agers continued ushering in the age of "peace and harmony."

THUMP!

"Did you see that?" Sean cried. "The way she got that guy with her sign."

SMACK!

"And check out that guy over there!" Melissa shouted. "He's really dangerous with that crystal necklace."

WHACK!

Another soldier dropped to the ground. His head had busted through a sign that read, *Show us your love* and *Share your peace.*

And then, just when things were really getting out of control, a loud, booming voice came from the direction of the lights.

"Three . . . two . . . one. *Roll 'em!*"

The fighting stopped in mid-punch.

"They're getting ready to attack!" one of the soldiers shouted.

"They're going to leave without us!" a New Ager cried.

Just as suddenly as the fighting had begun, it stopped. Now everyone was scrambling up the hill, trying to see what would happen.

Sean and Melissa were somewhere in the middle of the crowd as Sean turned to his sister and asked, " 'Roll 'em'—is that an outer-space term?"

Melissa shook her head. "I don't know."

As they drew closer to the bright lights, they could make out two round silver something-or-others. They seemed to be floating six or seven feet above the ground. Just a few yards beyond them were the blinding lights. And standing in the middle, between the silver circles and the lights, was a mysterious figure. It's back was turned to them, and the lights were so bright that they couldn't make out any of its details.

Sean's heart pounded so hard that it made his whole body shake. Was he really going to come face-to-face with a being from another planet? Were they finally going to—

KA-BLAM!

Sean's heart skipped a beat.

KA-BLAM! KA-BLAM!

Sean's heart skipped two beats.

He spun around to see one of the soldiers deciding to shoot first and ask questions later. So far all he had managed to do was rip a hole in one of the silver something-or-others.

"Look out!" a voice from inside the lights shouted.

"Someone's shooting at us! They shot a hole in my reflector!"

The mysterious figure spun around, and Sean immediately recognized her. It was Barbie Waters, the TV reporter! And she was angry in a major way.

"Put down those guns!" she shouted. "Are you people nuts?"

One of the soldiers stepped forward. "Barbie Waters," he said, "I shoulda known it would be you!"

"Shoulda known it would be me . . . what?" Barbie demanded.

"In cahoots with the Martians."

"In cahoots with . . . what are you talking about?"

"I've been watching you a long time," the soldier said. "I know what you've been up to." He turned to the rest of the group. "Ya see these round things . . . these, what'd they call them? Reflectors?"

The group nodded.

"These ain't reflectors," he continued. "These here are signaling devices."

"Signaling devices?" Barbie shouted. "You're crazy! We're taping a story for the evening news. These reflectors are just part of our equipment." She grabbed the one without the hole and held it high over her head. "You hold it up like this, see . . . and use it to reflect the light so that it fills in the shadows and—"

"Look out!" the soldier yelled. "She's signaling for the attack to begin!"

A dozen of the wannabes hit the ground with their guns ready to fire, while Ramma Lamma and a dozen of her followers ran to Barbie and banged their tambourines. A few even grabbed the reflector out of her hands and began stroking its shiny surface, hoping to experience its "mystical" powers.

"I'm telling you," Barbie shouted over the noise and confusion. "I have nothing to do with Martians! I'm a reporter. I'm just doing my job!"

The New Agers crowded in, reaching out to touch her clothes, her skin . . . anything to experience what they hoped would be a "close encounter."

Farther up the hill Slobs was racing back to Sean and Melissa. She had just made an important discovery and was anxious to let them know. But her nose had suddenly picked up another delicious scent. And as with most scents, it was just too good to pass up. She dropped her nose to the ground and continued to sniff when, suddenly, it touched something very, very wet. How fascinating. Now the scent was stuck to her nose. It was so strong that it made her sneeze. She tried to wipe it off on the ground, but it wouldn't go away.

She leaned over to a nearby tuft of grass and tried wiping it off.

No success.

Next, she tried rubbing her nose in a pile of leaves.

Ditto in the success department. Nothing seemed to work. Her nose was still wet, and the smell was so strong that it made her eyes water. She had to do something. But what? Finally, in frustration, she leaned back her head and let loose a long and mournful . . .

HOWLLLL.

"Listen," Melissa said to Sean. "Did you hear that?"

"It's Slobs."

The two of them scanned the hilltop. "It sounds like she's over there."

"Let's go!" Sean cried.

They left the crowd behind and started up the hill. They were heading in the direction of Roy and Larry's when Sean spotted something in the darkness. "Hey, check it out."

Melissa saw it, too. A huge circle burned into the grass and weeds. "Is it . . . is it a landing site?" she asked.

Sean stooped down for a closer look. "Could be. Whatever it is, I'd say we're definitely on to something."

Melissa gave a little shiver. "I'd feel a lot safer if Slobs were here."

"Me too." Sean rose and the two of them continued making their way up the hill. It was already dark, and they traveled slowly . . . carefully—until suddenly—

"Ow!"

Sean spun to Melissa. "What's wrong?"

She was on the ground, holding her ankle. "My foot! I twisted it."

Sean dropped to his knees to check it out. "Are you sure?" he asked. "I mean, it's not broken or anything, is it?"

But at that moment, Melissa was no longer thinking of her foot. Instead, she was staring straight ahead and trying to speak. "S-s-s-sean . . ." she stuttered.

He glanced at her, then looked over his shoulder.

He wished he hadn't.

For just behind him, a small, glowing orb was speeding toward them. It was less than fifty feet away— and quickly closing in.

"What is it?" Melissa cried.

Sean swallowed hard, trying to find his voice. "Maybe it's one of those little spacecrafts Larry told us about."

"Or some sort of missile they're firing at us!" Melissa cried.

It continued streaking toward them . . . twenty feet away . . .

Fifteen . . .

Ten . . .

"What do we do?" Melissa screamed. "What do we do?"

8

As Plain as the Nose on Your Face

THURSDAY, 18:09 PDST

The tiny UFO raced toward Sean and Melissa. There was no time to run, no place to hide. They ducked, covering their heads with their arms, bracing for impact, fearing the worst.

And then it hit.

But it wasn't exactly what they expected. Instead of blasting a hole through them, or crashing into them, it leaped on them. And instead of cold, hard metal, or a fancy death ray, it was wet, mushy, and hairy. It also had the worse case of dog breath they had ever smelled.

"Sean?" Melissa asked.

"Yes, Misty?"

"Are UFOs supposed to lick your face?"

"I don't think so."

It was about this time that Melissa opened her eyes. And it was about this time that she yelled, "Slobs! What are you doing here?"

It was true. The tiny UFO was Slobs. Or at least part of Slobs . . . the nose part, to be exact. It was glowing like a light bulb.

Melissa reached up and hugged the dog. "She must have heard me yell when I twisted my ankle. Good girl! Good dog!" Melissa patted her hard on the side. "You're always trying to protect us, aren't you?"

Sean joined in the hugs. "What happened, girl?" he asked. "What happened to your nose?"

Slobs let out a little whine.

Sean turned to his sister. "Can I borrow your handkerchief?"

"What for?"

"I want to find out what's on Slobs' nose."

"You wanna use *my* handkerchief to wipe *her* nose?"

"Of course."

Melissa looked at him like he had a screw loose. "What about you—don't you have a tissue or something?"

Sean let out a sigh of frustration. Girls—they could be so fussy sometimes. Without a word, he reached down, pulled out his shirttail, and began rubbing it on the dog's nose. As he did a small portion of the shirt began to glow.

He pulled the shirt to his own nose and gave it a sniff. "It's paint," he said. "Glow-in-the-dark paint!"

"Are you sure?" Melissa asked.

"Here. Take a whiff." He pulled his shirt in her direction.

She leaned away. "Uh . . . no, thanks. I'll take your word for it. But how did Slobs get glow-in-the-dark paint all over her nose?"

"She must have been tracking something and bumped into it."

"But what's glow-in-the-dark paint doing way out—" Suddenly Melissa stopped. "Wait a minute."

"Are you thinking what I'm thinking?" Sean asked.

Melissa began to nod. "I'm thinking that these glowing UFOs that people have been seeing . . ."

". . . may have had a little help from a fresh paint job," Sean concluded.

"Remember what Dad said?" Melissa asked. "How ninety-five percent of all UFO sightings have a natural explanation?"

"But just because the UFO has been painted doesn't

mean it's not from outer space," Sean argued. "Maybe it got dirty on the trip here."

"Maybe . . . or maybe there's a natural explanation for all the clues we've been finding."

"Natural?" Sean asked. "What about those strange voices on Mr. Carlson's television?"

"I don't know. Maybe it's just some people talking on a CB—or on a short-wave radio or something. Maybe Mr. Carlson's old TV set just happens to be picking them up."

As much as he hated to admit it, Sean agreed Melissa was starting to make sense. "You might have a point. I've even heard of people picking up radio signals with fillings in their teeth. But . . ."

"But what?" Melissa asked.

"Mr. Carlson said he saw the flying saucer go right over his house. What about that?"

"And he also found Bigfoot's footprints in his backyard and ran into Elvis Presley at the 7–11."

"Kmart," Sean corrected. "But you're right. You know, you're becoming quite the detective."

Melissa looked up at him, obviously waiting for a zinger to follow. But there was none. "Really?" she asked.

He nodded. "And I think we're beginning to make a great team."

Even in the darkness he could see his little sister blush with pleasure . . . and it made him feel good. Of course, he wouldn't want to make a habit of complimenting her. After all, she was his sister. But still . . .

He knelt down to scratch Slobs behind the ears. "And you're a good detective, too," he said. "In fact . . . I'll bet you're the only one who really knows what's going on around here, aren't you?"

The big dog whined.

"What do you think she wants?" Melissa asked.

As if answering, Slobs jumped up, ran a short distance up the path, then turned around and began barking at them.

"She wants us to follow her," Sean said.

"Follow her? In the dark?"

"Yeah, kind of like a Rudolph thing."

"Rudolph?"

"You know. The red-nosed reindeer." He started to sing, " 'Rudolph with your nose so bright, won't you . . .' "

Melissa winced, and Slobs began to howl. (Sean was no Frank Sinatra.)

" '. . . guide my sleigh tonight—' "

"All right," Melissa groaned. "We get the picture."

Sean stopped his singing, and Slobs stopped her howling. Once again the dog began running around in circles and barking.

"She really does want to show us something," Sean shouted over the noise. "How's your foot?"

Melissa tested it out. "It's a little stiff, but it'll be okay."

"Good. Let's go."

Slobs took off, and they followed right behind.

"Her nose is just as good as a flashlight," Melissa shouted.

"Better," Sean answered. "She doesn't need batteries."

As they approached the top of the rise, they began to hear faint humming and hammering. Soon flickering lights came into view. First red. Then blue. Then white.

They continued . . . around the trees, through the grass, into the—ouch!—thorny bushes. The flickering lights grew brighter and the noises grew louder. Now they could hear electrical sounds—the whining of power tools . . . and more hammering. Lots and lots of hammering.

At last they reached the top of the rise. There was Slobs, sitting in front of them. She was on the edge of a small cliff, wagging her tail as she looked down at the activity below.

Sean motioned for Melissa to stoop low and be quiet. She nodded. By the time they got to the dog, they were practically crawling. And when they looked down . . . well, they couldn't believe their eyes.

Spread out below them were at least a dozen cars. Maybe more. To be more accurate, they were pieces of cars. Some without wheels. Others missing doors and fenders. Still others had their hoods open.

Several men with cutting torches and other tools worked feverishly, cutting engine parts and other pieces out of the cars. In their bright orange coveralls and welding face masks, they almost looked like spacemen.

Almost.

Sean turned to Melissa. "Cutting torches? That explains the flickering lights."

Melissa nodded as they watched a large man walk among the workers. "Hurry up!" he shouted. "We've gotta wrap this thing up tonight and get out of here!"

"Look!" Melissa pointed down into the darkness.

Sean strained to see.

"It's a Saturn," she said.

"A what?"

"That blue car over there. It's a Saturn!"

Sean's mouth fell open. "You're right!" He searched the other cars. "And that white station wagon over there . . . that's a Ford Galaxy. And there's a Mercury! They weren't talking about planets over the TV!" he exclaimed. "They were talking about . . ."

Melissa joined him. ". . . *cars!* These guys aren't invaders from space—they're car thieves!"

"I've heard about places like this," Sean said. "It's called a chop shop. People steal cars, then they cut them up and sell the parts. They can make a lot of money that way."

He started to rise. "Come on!" he whispered. "We've got to get the police."

BRRRRP! BRRRRP!

Oh no—the cell phone. He grabbed it, and as quietly as possible whispered, "Hello?"

"How are you two doing?" the voice on the other end asked.

"It's Mr. Carlson," Sean whispered to his sister. "Listen, Mr. Carlson, I can't talk right now. I'll call you back."

He quickly closed the phone. "I hope nobody heard that!"

Unfortunately, somebody had. Because as he turned

to go, he found their path blocked by two very familiar figures.

"Well, well, if it ain't our ol' friends . . . and their wunder dog, Suds."

"Roy!" Sean cried. "Larry!" He fought back the panic and tried to sound more casual. "So . . . how are you guys doing?"

Melissa joined in, also trying to sound calm and nonchalant. "Nice night for a walk, isn't it?"

The men said nothing.

"We're, uh . . ." Sean's mind raced for an excuse. "We're just getting our dog some exercise."

Still no response.

"Well," Sean started to pass, "I guess we'll be going now."

Larry shoved a rifle into Sean's chest. "I guess you won't."

Sean came to a stop. For a moment no one moved.

Finally Roy spoke. "You two ain't goin' nowhere."

9

Invasion of the Whackos

THURSDAY, 18:33 PDST

"Larry!" Roy shouted. "Look out!"

Larry spun around to see Slobs running straight at him. She leaped into the air, but he ducked. Instead of hitting him, she went flying right over his head! And when she landed, she didn't stop. She just kept on running down the hill.

Larry raised his gun toward her and fired. . . .

KA-BLEWY!

The bullet whizzed just above her head and hit a rock, causing sparks to fly.

"Stop it!" Melissa cried. She took aim at Larry's left shin, but Roy grabbed her before she got in the kick.

Larry prepared to shoot again, but Slobs' glowing

nose disappeared into the bushes. He lowered his gun. "That dog of yers is some kinda coward, ain't she? Running off like a scairt rabbit soon as she saw you was in trouble."

"She's probably going to get the police," Sean said.

"Oh sure," Roy laughed. "You must think we're perfect fools."

"No, sir," Sean replied. "Nobody's perfect."

Larry took off his *Worm Farm* hat and scratched his head. "Did he just insult us?"

"I dunno. If he did, I didn't get it."

"Well . . . that's enough chitchat." Larry pulled a walkie-talkie out of his hip pocket and raised the antenna. "Little Green Man calling Mothership. Little Green Man calling Mothership!"

Now Melissa and Sean both realized where they'd heard the mysterious TV voice. It had been Larry all along.

"This is Mothership. Come in, Little Green Man!"

"We got 'em."

"You have them?" the other voice answered. "Excellent! Everything is going according to plan. You know what to do."

"Yes, sir." Larry lowered the antenna and put the

walkie-talkie back into his pocket. "Come on, you two. We got big plans fer you."

Several hundred yards down the hill, the wannabe soldiers and their New Age friends were finally convinced that Barbie Waters was not an alien Martian. That's when they heard Larry's shot.

KA-BLEWY . . . Blewy . . . blewy . . .

The noise echoed through the hills.

"What was that?!" a soldier yelled.

"Gunfire!" Ramma Lamma shouted. "Someone's shooting at them!"

"Shooting at *them*?" Frank shouted. "*They're* shooting at us! The invasion has begun!"

With that, another half dozen of his men threw down their guns and ran for home.

"Come on," Frank shouted, "we've got to stop them!"

"Come on," Ramma Lamma shouted, "we've got to save them!"

And so the mob started up the hill.

Meanwhile, Mr. Carlson paced back and forth in his living room. He knew something was wrong. He just had that feeling. Sean had hung up on him so rudely, and it wasn't like the Hunter kids to be rude. And what was it that Little Green Man had just said over his TV? Something about "we got 'em"? Could he have been talking about the kids?

Mr. Carlson looked at the TV. Nothing but Vanna White choosing letters on *Wheel of Fortune*. Just a moment ago the outer-space people had been talking up a storm. Now there was nothing.

He looked out the window for the four hundred and seventeenth time. And for the four hundred and seventeenth time there was nothing . . . nothing except a little, glowing ball heading down the street, bouncing up and down as it approached.

What on earth?

Mr. Carlson wasn't as scared as he was curious, so he rushed out into the front yard for a better look. Yes . . . it was a strange, glowing ball. No doubt some sort of probe from the Mothership. But what was that dog doing directly behind it?

No, wait. The dog wasn't chasing it. The dog was . . . wearing it? And as it came closer, Mr. Carlson recognized her.

"Slobs," he cried, "is that you?"

But Slobs didn't stop. She kept right on running, right past Mr. Carlson and right on down the street.

"What have they done to you?" Mr. Carlson shouted. "What have those monsters done to your nose?"

But even now, scarier thoughts ran through his head. If they'd done that to the dog, who knows what they'd done to the kids!

Mr. Carlson hobbled back inside, picked up the phone, and quickly dialed up their father's radio station.

The phone rang several times before someone answered.

"Good evening, KRZY."

"Hello . . . this is Ben Carlson, and I—"

"Oh hello, Mr. Carlson." It was Herbie, the station's goofy engineer. They had talked several times before. Actually, several times that week. "What is it this time?" Herbie asked. "Has a werewolf been running through your backyard again?"

"No! Not a werewolf!" Mr. Carlson snapped impatiently. "Just a dog with a glowing nose, and—"

"A dog with a glowing nose? Oh well, I really wouldn't worry about it. We have a lot of them in Midvale this time of year. Say . . . you haven't seen Elvis lately, have you?"

"Listen, Herbie," Mr. Carlson tried to keep his voice even. "I guess maybe I've made a few strange phone calls in my time—"

"Oh, a couple," Herbie chuckled. "Last I heard they were putting your picture in *The Guiness Book of World Records*."

"But I saw a dog running by here! And her nose was glowing, and she was . . . she was . . ."

Herbie was no longer paying attention. He was too busy spilling hot coffee all over his pants. (I forgot to mention, Ol' Herb doesn't have the best coordination in the world—to be honest, he doesn't have *any* coordination.) "Thank you, Mr. Carlson," he said, jumping around the room. "I'll make a report of that. One dog with a glowing nose."

"But it's the Hunter kids' dog. And I think they're in terrible—"

"Thank you, Mr. Carlson. We appreciate the tip. Good-bye." With that, he hung up.

Mr. Carlson pulled the receiver from his ear and simply stared at it. It was no use. No one would believe him.

But he had to do something.

Back on the hill, Sean and Melissa were pushed and shoved through the darkness.

"Where are you taking us?" Sean demanded.

"Don't worry," Roy answered. "You'll be findin' out soon 'nuff."

Larry gave Sean another shove, and Roy did the same to Melissa.

"Ow!" she complained. "You're messing up my hair!"

"Yer hair?" Roy laughed. "You got a lot more to be frettin' about than yer hair!"

"Yeah?" Sean demanded. "Like what?"

"Like that thing right thar!"

Sean turned, and both he and Melissa gasped in surprise. Directly in front of them, sitting in a little clearing, was a flying saucer. It glowed in the dark and was about ten feet across. It looked exactly like the UFO in the picture Roy and Larry had shown on TV. Beside it were two men. The first was standing. He was tall with greasy black hair and a beak of a nose. The other man was sitting. He wore orange coveralls, a welding face mask. . . . and his hands and feet were tied!

"Here they are, Mr. Miller," Larry called. "We got 'em . . . just like we tole you."

"Good work, boys." The first man stepped forward. "So . . . you two are the brains behind the Bloodhounds

119

Detective Agency. Well, your snooping around here has caused me quite a bit of trouble." He broke into a sinister grin. "But that's okay, because now I'm going to make some trouble for you."

Sean and Melissa exchanged frightened glances.

Sean swallowed nervously. "Is that . . . is that really a spaceship?"

"Spaceship?" Miller threw back his head and laughed. "I guess we did a better job on this flying saucer than I thought!" He knocked on the side of the metal. "We made this baby from leftover junk. After all, we needed at least *one* flying saucer to keep you people from figuring out what we're *really* doing up here!"

"So that's it!" Melissa exclaimed. "When the people in town saw the light from your torches, they thought they were seeing a UFO!"

"We simply gave them what they wanted." Miller tapped the metal again. "That way they could go around chasing flying saucers and talking about Martians—"

"While you were stealing all the cars in town," Sean concluded.

Miller laughed. "Very good, kid. But not all the cars. Just the ones we wanted." Suddenly his smile faded. "And everything would have been fine if it weren't for you two . . . and our little soldier boy, here." He reached down to the tied-up man and ripped off his welding helmet.

Sean and Melissa caught their breath. It was Bear's father!

"Mr. Thompson!" Melissa cried. "Are you all right!"

The man tried to answer, but it was impossible with the tape sealed across his mouth.

Suddenly Mr. Miller's walkie-talkie crackled to life. "Mothership, this is Blue Moon. Come in, Mothership."

Mr. Miller answered, "Mothership here."

"The crowd of people are heading this way, sir!"

"That's all right," Miller said. "We're almost ready for them. Now, here's what I want you to do. . . ."

While Mr. Miller was talking, Sean leaned over and whispered to his sister, "I wonder if Old Man Carlson is hearing their conversation over his TV?"

Melissa nodded. "If only there was a way to get a message to him and let him know that we're in trouble."

Sean tapped his wristwatch with his finger and smiled at her.

"Jeremiah?" she whispered.

He nodded.

"What are you two whispering about?" Mr. Miller demanded.

"Oh nothing," Sean said. "Just how it would be nice

121

if we had a little . . . er . . . alien friend who could help us."

"That's right," Melissa added, a little more loudly. "You know . . . a little alien friend named . . . oh . . . *Jeremiah* . . . or something like that . . . who could somehow let Mr. Carlson know that we're in trouble and—"

"What are you saying?" Miller snapped.

"Maybe they're crazy with fear," suggested Larry.

"Yeah," said Roy. "Look at the way they keep talkin' into his wristwatch. Crazy with fear can make ya do that."

"Whatever," Miller growled. He then turned to the kids and bowed deeply. "I wish we could chat longer, but as you've just heard, we're running out of time. Roy . . . Larry . . . why don't you show our two guests what wonderful parting gifts we have for them?"

"Sure thing, boss."

Roy and Larry stepped behind the flying saucer and came back with two more welding helmets, a couple pairs of orange overalls, and some handcuffs.

"How about that?" Miller said. "We seem to have two extra space suits! Now, I would appreciate it if you would put them on."

"Space suits?" Sean asked.

"Put 'em on!" Miller barked.

Sean and Melissa obeyed. The suits didn't fit perfectly
. . . but they were perfect enough. And the welding
helmets added the finishing touch. In just a couple of
minutes, the two looked like tourists from a neighboring
solar system.

"Ah." Miller smiled. "If I didn't know better, I'd
swear you had just dropped in from the Crab Nebula . . .
or maybe Orion."

"We look stupid," Sean said. "And whatever you're
planning . . . it's never going to work."

"Oh, but it will," Miller grinned. "We'll take off and
leave you behind as a decoy. Mr. Thompson's friends will
spot you, think they've discovered aliens, and surround
you . . . while we make a clean getaway."

"And if yer lucky," Larry said, "they won't shoot first
and ask questions later."

"He's right," Roy agreed. "It'd be a shame to get
those beautiful space suits all filled with holes."

"And if you *should* happen to survive," Miller added,
"be sure to tell Midvale thanks for the cars . . . and the
money." Then turning to Larry, he asked, "Have you
readied the sound effects?"

Larry nodded eagerly. "All we gotta do is turn on the
speakers, and they'll think the invasion has begun."

"Excellent," Miller sneered. "So what are we waiting for? Start it up and let's get going!"

The wannabe soldiers and the New Agers made their way up the hill through the darkness when they suddenly heard

RAOWW-RAOWW-RAOWW.

"What is it?" Ramma Lamma cried.

"Could be the spaceship!" Frank shouted. "Come on, let's hurry!"

The mob raced up the ridge as the noise grew louder and louder, and louder some more. After several more moments, they finally reached the top and were able to look down into the small clearing.

"It's the flying saucer!" Ramma Lamma cried.

"And look at them orange creatures standing beside it!" Frank shouted.

"They're the Martians!" someone yelled.

"They're leaving without telling us their secret to

inner peace!" Ramma Lamma cried. "We can't let them leave!"

"They're not going anywhere," Frank shouted as he raised his rifle. He lined up his sights on one of the orange creatures . . . and prepared to fire. . . .

10

Wrapping up

THURSDAY, 19:05 PDST

KA-BLEWY!

"They're firing at us!" Melissa screamed.

"Don't shoot!" Sean shouted. "We're friendly!"

Unfortunately, there was some good news and some bad news. . . .

The bad news was that the welding masks over their faces made it impossible for anybody to hear them.

The good news was that Frank and the other soldiers weren't such great shots. (The fact that Ramma Lamma and her buddies were jumping on their backs, beating them with their fists, and pulling their hair certainly helped.)

KA-BLEWY!

The second shot whizzed just over Sean's right shoulder. He tried to run—but being handcuffed to the flying saucer made it a little difficult.

"What's the matter with these guys?" Sean yelled. "Can't they see we're tied up!"

KA-BLEWY!

"Guess not!" Melissa answered.

A third shot rang out, only this time it was immediately followed by a

KA-CHING!

as the bullet ricocheted off the spacecraft, and Sean fell to the ground.

"Sean!?" Melissa screamed. "Sean, are you all right??"

Sean lay sprawled out on the ground. At first he thought he'd been killed. But then, noticing that he was still breathing, he realized it might be something else.

Wait a minute . . . what was he doing sprawled out on the ground? Hadn't he just been handcuffed to the flying saucer? He glanced at the handcuffs and had his answer. They were broken! The bullet had hit them, and now he was free!

Sean leaped to his feet and looked both directions.

"Look out!" someone yelled. "One of 'em is getting away!"

KA-BLEWY!

The next shot hit a branch above his head, missing him by a mile. But for some reason, Sean had this sudden urge to begin running for his life.

KA-BLEWY!

Another shot knocked the tail feathers from an owl, who flew off screeching in anger.

"Run!" Melissa yelled. "Run, Sean, run!"

He didn't have to be told twice. It wasn't easy running in the "space suit," but he was determined to keep going. As long as they were chasing him, he knew Melissa would be safe.

KA-BLEWY! KA-BLEWY!

"Help us, Lord!" he prayed. "Please, help. . . ."

Ben Carlson was back on the phone. Now he was trying to get the police to believe him.

"No!" he shouted. "I haven't seen Elvis lately, and I—"

Suddenly his TV began to act up:

HISSSSSS! CRACKLE. . . .

Carlson stopped in midsentence. He turned to his set . . . then he dropped the phone to the floor.

There on his television was a spaceman! (Either that or Pat Sajack was dressing up for St. Patrick's Day.)

Mr. Carlson moved closer. Funny! This guy looked more like a leprechaun than a spaceman. I mean, he was all green . . . no, he was red . . . make that blue. Whatever he was, he kept changing colors.

And he was trying to talk. . . .

Mr. Carlson moved closer, placing his ear next to the speaker. He could just barely hear the words.

". . . Vid . . . eee . . . oh. . . . Camaro."

What in the world was a . . . *videeoh Camaro?"*

Mr. Hunter was just pulling into the driveway, coming home from the station, when he spotted Slobs running toward him.

"Slobs! What are you doing out?"

"Woof!"

"What's the matter, girl? Did Sean forget to feed you?"

"Woof!"

Dad looked in the direction of the house. Not a single light was on inside.

"Where are the kids, girl?"

"Woof!"

He looked back at the dog. "And why is your nose glowing? WHY IS YOUR NOSE GLOWING!"

Slobs began running in tight little circles, still barking.

"What is it, girl? Are the kids in trouble?"

"WOOF! WOOF! WOOF!"

"Okay! Let's go!"

Dad jumped back in the car. He started the engine and followed Slobs up the street toward the hills.

Suddenly Mr. Carlson had it. "Video camera?" he shouted at the TV. "Is that what you're saying . . . 'video camera'?"

The little electronic character began jumping up and down in excitement.

With shaking hands, Ben Carlson picked up the video camera Sean and Melissa had left behind—the one they had attached to his television set. *Now . . . which button was I supposed to push? This one?*

CLICK!

orreee-orreee-Orreee-ORREEE-ORREEE.

Oh no! What was happening?

ORREEE-ORREEE-ORREEE-ORREEE . . .

Mr. Carlson felt so strange! And he seemed to be . . . EXPANDING!

"AUGH! IT'S A MONSTER!" Frank screamed and pointed at the sky.

Everyone stopped and looked up . . . including Sean.

A hideous monster towered high above and stared down at them. He was awful! Absolutely hideous! He had bugged-out eyes. Crooked, yellow teeth. And the wildest hair you've ever seen. Hair that seemed to be . . .

Wait a minute. Sean rubbed his eyes. That huge

monster in the sky . . . it looked exactly like . . . it *was* Mr. Carlson!

Mr. Carlson had no idea what had happened. One moment he was fiddling with the video camera. The next, he was ninety feet tall and stumbling around kicking over trees!

"Where am I?" he shouted. "And who's doing all that screaming down there?"

"IT'S A GIANT ALIEN COME TO EAT US!" another wannabe soldier screamed. Panic swept the crowd, and soon everyone was screaming their heads off.

Well, everyone but Sean. He'd realized Jeremiah had gotten their message. Apparently the little guy had contacted Mr. Carlson and convinced him to try Doc's 3-D holographic video camera. And apparently the bugs in the invention still weren't completely worked out.

Suddenly Sean heard shouting and crying from behind the ridge. Shouting and crying that sounded an awful lot like it belonged to Larry and Roy.

"Help us!"

"Don't let him eat us!"

Larry was the first to appear over the ridge, immediately followed by Roy, then Mr. Miller, and several other men, all with their arms held high.

"We give up!" Mr. Miller yelled. "Just don't hurt us! Please don't let that monster hurt us!"

And then, as if answering their pleas, the Ben Carlson monster began to

POP . . . CRACKLE-CRACKLE-CRACKLE . . .
FIZZLE . . .

"*What-at-ats hap-hap-happening?!*" he cried.

Most of the New Agers lifted their hands and began to chant. . . .

Most of the wannabes dropped their guns and began to run. . . .

And suddenly Mr. Carlson disappeared. Just like that. His holographic image had completely vanished and he was gone.

"Will somebody please tell me what's going on?" Frank demanded.

"I'm sorry!" Larry blubbered. "I didn't wanna steal no cars! It's all Roy's fault!"

"My fault?" Roy shouted. "Mr. Miller here, he's the head of it . . . we jes' wanted to make a lettle extra money!"

"Will you two shut up!" Miller shouted. (Now that the monster was gone, he was feeling a little braver.) But he was too late. Roy and Larry were so scared that they didn't stop talking until they'd confessed everything.

But it wasn't completely over. Not yet. . . .

Mr. Miller still had his gun . . . and that nasty personality of his. With one swift move, he pulled Melissa to him, yanked off her helmet, and pointed his revolver at her head. "Everybody stand back—or the girl gets it! You!" He pointed at Frank. "Give me your car keys. And, Larry, get over here and unlock this girl's handcuffs."

Frank nodded. He dug into his pocket, pulled out his keys, and tossed them to the man.

Larry bumbled forward and nervously obeyed.

Sean stood nearby, desperate to save his sister. But unsure how.

Then he spotted something coming up the other side of the hill. It was directly behind Mr. Miller. Something that looked like a small, glowing ball of light.

Mr. Miller continued his bad-guy sneering. "I'd like to say it's been a pleasure doing business with you, but—"

Sean could see the light clearly now. It was Slobs . . . with her glow-in-the-dark nose. And Dad was running right behind her, his flashlight cutting through the darkness. They were closing in fast as Miller continued his speech. "But it has not been a pleasure. In fact, you people are the worst excuse for—"

That's when Slobs leaped into the air. Her aim was perfect as she landed . . . right in the middle of Mr. Miller's back.

"OAFF!"

The gun flew from his hand as he fell to the ground, with Slobs on top, growling and biting for all she was worth.

"Help!" Miller shouted. "Get her off me! Get her off!"

Sean didn't particularly want to help, not after all the problems Mr. Miller had caused. But he figured he better call Slobs off . . . after all, who knew what type of indigestion she could get by chewing on someone so mean.

"Come on, Slobs. Come on, girl! That a girl . . . *good* girl . . . good girl."

FRIDAY, 07:30 PDST

Morning came peacefully to Midvale. It was going to be a great day. It was especially going to be great over at Sean and Melissa's.

Because at that particular moment, they were sitting with Dad at the breakfast table and enjoying the morning headlines. . . .

YOUNG DETECTIVES SMASH CAR-THEFT RING

"Check it out," Sean said. He cleared his throat and, in an overdramatic voice, read the article: " 'Melissa and Sean Hunter, with the help of their dog, Slobbers, and one Benjamin P. Carlson, heroically broke up an auto-theft ring that had stolen more than seventy-five cars in Midvale and several other communities throughout the state.' "

"All right!" Melissa grinned.

Dad looked over the table at them and beamed. "You guys had quite the adventure, didn't you?"

"You can say that again!" Melissa said.

"Okay . . . you guys had quite the—"

"Dad! That's just a figure of speech."

Dad chuckled as Sean turned to him. "I've been wondering about something."

137

"What's that, son?"

"Ramma Lamma . . . and all those New Age people?"

"What about them?"

"Well . . . when it turned out that the alien space thing wasn't real . . . it was like they didn't want to believe it. I mean . . . she was kind of mad at us and kept saying there really were space people in Midvale."

Dad nodded. "Yes, I heard her carrying on."

"Why was she making such a big deal about it?"

Dad gave a long, low sigh. "Well . . . the Bible talks about folks like that. People who are always looking for a new teacher . . . some enlightened one . . . anything so they don't have to listen to God's Word."

"Why?" Melissa asked.

Dad shook his head. "Scripture puts it this way: 'They have said no to the Truth; they have refused to believe it and love it and let it save them, so God will allow them to believe lies with all their hearts.'"

"That's terrible," Melissa said.

Dad nodded. "But that's how some people are. There's nothing you can do to get them to believe the truth if they don't want to. . . ."

Silence hung over the table. It was true—they'd seen this sort of thing during the entire case. People believed what they wanted—whether it was the New Agers or the wannabe soldiers. Each group had its own beliefs and neither wanted to be confused with the facts.

"But you two . . ." Dad looked over at them and smiled. "I'm really proud that you didn't let yourself get carried away and that you stuck to the facts."

Sean nodded and Melissa shrugged.

"Well, most of the time," she admitted.

"But you know what makes me the proudest?"

"The fact that we're so good-looking?" Sean asked.

Dad shot him a look.

Sean shrugged.

"What makes me the proudest is that you were both so nice to Mr. Carlson."

"Mr. Carlson's not a bad guy," Melissa said. "He's really pretty cool."

"That's right," Sean agreed. "Besides, if it wasn't for him, we wouldn't have solved the case."

Dad nodded. "Well, I'm glad you were kind. I know that being kind can sometimes be a nuisance, but—"

BRRRP! BRRRP!

Sean reached into his pocket and pulled out his cellular. "Hello? Oh hi, Mr. Carlson."

Melissa and Dad exchanged looks.

"What's that you say? Eating your lawn? Are you—

yes, but did you? I know, but is it? Yes, sir. We'll be right over."

Sean sighed, and his shoulders seemed to droop a little as he shut off the phone.

"What's up?" Melissa asked.

"It's Mr. Carlson," Sean said. "Seems there's a dinosaur in his backyard."

"A *what*?"

"A dinosaur," Sean repeated. "And he wants us to come over to help him catch it!"

Dad broke into a quiet chuckle. Slobs thumped her tail in anticipation. And Melissa sat back and covered her eyes. "Oh no," she groaned, "here we go again. . . ."

By **Bill Myers**

Children's Series:
Bloodhounds, Inc. — mystery/comedy
McGee and Me! — book and video
The Incredible Worlds of Wally McDoogle — comedy

Teen Series:
Forbidden Doors

Adult Novels:
Blood of Heaven
Threshold
Fire of Heaven

Nonfiction:
Christ B.C.
The Dark Side of the Supernatural
Hot Topics, Tough Questions
Faith Encounter

Picture Books:
Baseball for Breakfast

Series for Middle Graders* From BHP

THE ACCIDENTAL DETECTIVES · by Sigmund Brouwer
Action-packed adventures lead Ricky Kidd and his friends into places they never dreamed of, drawing them closer with every step.

ADVENTURES DOWN UNDER · by Robert Elmer
When Patrick McWaid's father is unjustly sent to Australia as a prisoner in 1867, the rest of the family follows, uncovering action-packed mystery along the way.

ADVENTURES OF THE NORTHWOODS · by Lois Walfrid Johnson
Kate O'Connell and her stepbrother Anders encounter mystery and adventure in northwest Wisconsin near the turn of the century.

BLOODHOUNDS, INC. · by Bill Myers
Hilarious, hair-raising suspense follows brother-and-sister detectives Sean and Melissa Hunter in these madcap mysteries with a message.

GIRLS ONLY! · by Beverly Lewis
Four talented young athletes become fast friends as together they pursue their Olympic dreams.

MANDIE BOOKS · by Lois Gladys Leppard
With over five million sold, the turn-of-the-century adventures of Mandie and her many friends will keep readers eager for more.

PROMISE OF ZION · by Robert Elmer
Following WWII, thirteen-year-old Dov Zalinsky leaves for Palestine—the one place he may still find his parents—and meets the adventurous Emily Parkinson. Together they experience the dangers of life in the Holy Land.

THE RIVERBOAT ADVENTURES · by Lois Walfrid Johnson
Libby Norstad and her friend Caleb face the challenges and risks of working with the Underground Railroad during the mid–1800s.

TRAILBLAZER BOOKS · by Dave and Neta Jackson
Follow the exciting lives of real-life Christian heroes through the eyes of child characters as they share their faith with others around the world.

THE YOUNG UNDERGROUND · by Robert Elmer
Peter and Elise Andersen's plots to protect their friends and themselves from Nazi soldiers in World War II Denmark guarantee fast-paced action and suspenseful reads.

*(ages 8–13)